St

A Freshly Baked Cozy Mystery

by

Kathleen Suzette

Books by Kathleen Suzette:

A Rainey Daye Cozy Mystery Series

Clam Chowder and a Murder
A Rainey Daye Cozy Mystery, book 1
A Short Stack and a Murder
A Rainey Daye Cozy Mystery, book 2
Cherry Pie and a Murder
A Rainey Daye Cozy Mystery, book 3
Barbecue and a Murder
A Rainey Daye Cozy Mystery, book 4
Birthday Cake and a Murder
A Rainey Daye Cozy Mystery, book 5
Hot Cider and a Murder
A Rainey Daye Cozy Mystery, book 6
Roast Turkey and a Murder
A Rainey Daye Cozy Mystery, book 7
Gingerbread and a Murder
A Rainey Daye Cozy Mystery, book 8
Fish Fry and a Murder
A Rainey Daye Cozy Mystery, book 9
Cupcakes and a Murder
A Rainey Daye Cozy Mystery, book 10
Lemon Pie and a Murder
A Rainey Daye Cozy Mystery, book 11
Pasta and a Murder
A Rainey Daye Cozy Mystery, book 12
Chocolate Cake and a Murder
A Rainey Daye Cozy Mystery, book 13

Pumpkin Spice Donuts and a Murder
A Rainey Daye Cozy Mystery, book 14
A Pumpkin Hollow Mystery Series
Candy Coated Murder
A Pumpkin Hollow Mystery, book 1
Murderously Sweet
A Pumpkin Hollow Mystery, book 2
Chocolate Covered Murder
A Pumpkin Hollow Mystery, book 3
Death and Sweets
A Pumpkin Hollow Mystery, book 4
Sugared Demise
A Pumpkin Hollow Mystery, book 5
Confectionately Dead
A Pumpkin Hollow Mystery, book 6
Hard Candy and a Killer
A Pumpkin Hollow Mystery, book 7
Candy Kisses and a Killer
A Pumpkin Hollow Mystery, book 8
Terminal Taffy
A Pumpkin Hollow Mystery, book 9
Fudgy Fatality
A Pumpkin Hollow Mystery, book 10
Truffled Murder
A Pumpkin Hollow Mystery, book 11
Caramel Murder
A Pumpkin Hollow Mystery, book 12
Peppermint Fudge Killer
A Pumpkin Hollow Mystery, book 13

A Gracie Williams Mystery, Book 1
Kicked the Bucket in Arizona,
A Gracie Williams Mystery, Book 2

A Home Economics Mystery Series

Appliqued to Death
A Home Economics Mystery, book 1

Table of Contents

Chapter One

MAY 27TH DAWNED CLEAR and bright. We traveled almost two hours to Sanford, Maine to compete in their annual Strawberry Festival Marathon. Alec drove while I dozed with a box of strawberry cupcakes in my lap. I, Allie McSwain, pastry baker extraordinaire, was running my first marathon and a marathon had never looked so terrifying. My best friend Lucy Gray and her husband Ed followed behind us in their car. The festival drew people from all over Maine, New Hampshire, and beyond and I figured I should make the most of it by renting a booth and selling my wares.

"You awake?" Alec asked with his sexy Maine accent.

I smiled but didn't open my eyes. "I love your accent. Have I ever told you that?"

He chuckled. "Maybe a time or two. We'll be there in about five minutes. You better open your eyes."

I groaned. I trained for this marathon for over a year, but now that the day was here, I was having serious doubts. I had intended to run the distance of 26.2 miles at least twice while in training, but it hurts to run that far. Yes, I wimped out, and I hoped I wouldn't regret it.

Right about now I was thinking I should have started with a half marathon, but I'm a Southern girl by birth and we don't do small. Besides that, we had registered and paid the entrance fee six months earlier. It was too late to cancel without forfeiting the money.

"I think I need a cupcake," I said, opening my eyes and sitting up. I could smell them through the closed box and I wasn't sure I could hold off much longer. Each cupcake had a dollop of strawberry filling and cream cheese in the center. Strawberry perfection.

"You've already eaten. You need to hold off," Alec said. His eyes were on the road, but he had a smirk on his lips.

I snorted. I never waited for food.

I took in the sights as Alec pulled into the fairgrounds. Booths lined a meandering sidewalk path down the middle of the fairgrounds, along with bounce houses and a huge blow-up slide for the kiddies. I could smell barbecues firing up and see huge silver pots set up for crab boils. My mouth watered. I wondered if we could skip the marathon and sit around eating all day instead.

"When we're done with the marathon, I am going to eat myself silly," I promised.

"That sounds like a plan," Alec said. "But aren't you worried about the calories?"

Alec was a tease.

"Calories schmalories. I'll burn a million of them running the marathon," I assured him. "Which booth are we?"

"Twenty-one," he said, pulling up to the back of the booth. An awning stretched across the top of the booth and a Maine flag was stuck in the corner.

I jumped out of the SUV as soon as we came to a stop and headed to the booth. The tabletop was bare wood and once it was covered with a tablecloth, it would be perfect for setting out the cupcakes. There were two folding chairs leaning against the booth and an outlet for electrical items. I had brought a small cash box and hoped I would have plenty of use for it.

The festival ran for a week and included the Memorial Day holiday. There would be large crowds looking for all kinds of strawberry things to buy, and it was the perfect opportunity to showcase my baked goods.

"Does the booth pass muster?" Alec asked, getting out of the car.

"It does," I said and set down the box of cupcakes. Other people were unloading trucks and cars into booths and I took in the sights. I had been to the Strawberry Festival several times, but that was more than ten years earlier and I had never been a vendor before. The weather was beautiful, and the atmosphere was festive and I was glad we were attending.

Lucy and Ed pulled their silver Volkswagen up next to Alec's car and parked.

"What do you make of it?" Lucy asked when she got out of the car. She had dyed her hair pink, and it peeked out from beneath the white baseball hat she wore.

"I think it looks good," I said. "We need to spread out those tablecloths."

"Got it," Ed said, picking up the folded red and white checked tablecloths I had brought.

Lucy took one from him and handed me an end, and we spread it out over the top of the table. There was a light breeze, threatening to blow the tablecloth off the table, so I put the box of cupcakes on top to hold it in place.

"Where do you want these?" Alec asked, carrying three more boxes of cupcakes.

"Space them out so they'll hold down the tablecloth," I said.

I brought brochures and business cards advertising my website and the fact that I sold baked goods at Henry's Home Cooking Restaurant in Sandy Harbor. I supposed not many people would make a two-hour drive for cupcakes, but I hoped someone might need a large order for a wedding or business event. If I could get a large enough order, I'd make the drive and deliver them myself.

"I need one of those cupcakes," Lucy said, lifting the lid on the box and inhaling. "I don't know how you come up with all the tasty desserts you make."

"There are mini cupcakes in that box over there," I said, pointing to the box. "We'll give those away so people can sample them and hopefully it will entice them to buy lots of regular sized ones."

Lucy helped herself to a mini cupcake, and I grabbed one, too.

"Mm," I groaned. I had outdone myself on these cupcakes. The cream cheese in the center was perfect with the strawberry filling.

"You can say that again," Lucy said, popping the second half of her mini cupcake into her mouth. "There may not be any sample cupcakes to give away if I'm not careful."

"We need to go check in and get our race bibs, Allie," Alec said. "How are you feeling?"

"Butterflies," I replied. My stomach felt like someone had released a cage full of squirrels in it and they were happy to be there. I had eaten before I left home and I had a handful of gels in case I got hungry along the route, but I wasn't sure how well I would do. It seemed like race day had come all too soon.

"Great. That means you're ready," Alec said. "Sugary cupcakes aren't going to do you any good. If you have to eat, try this." He handed me a strawberry protein bar.

I narrowed my eyes at him. My Alec was tall, dark and handsome, and true to his name, he was a smart aleck.

"I need to hit the ladies room before we go," I said, looking around. In my mind, I pictured myself desperately needing a bathroom and not being able to find one along the route. I dreaded having to drop my drawers in front of hundreds of innocent bystanders. It was inhumane.

"Over there," Alec said, pointing to a large building. "And there will be plenty of porta-potties along the race route. They've got you covered."

"That's a relief," I muttered.

We headed over as a stream of people wearing running gear went in and out of the bathrooms. My stomach dived bombed again, and I hoped I would make it.

I got in line with the female runners and waited my turn. Women around me chatted happily as if we were all about to hit

Macy's for their semi-annual lingerie sale. Was I the only person making herself sick with worry? I scanned the faces and caught sight of a woman that looked to be in her mid-twenties. She had long blond hair tied up with a braided pink shoestring and looked a little green around the gills. I smiled. A kindred spirit. I decided to stick close to her. Misery loves company, after all.

After I took care of business, I met Alec out in front of the bathrooms. Why is it that the line to the men's room moves at warp speed while the line for the ladies' room crawls at a snail's pace?

"Feeling okay?" he asked when I got to him.

I nodded.

"Let's go, then," Alec said.

We found the check-in booth and got in another line. People took their time, even though it was only forty-five minutes to start time, and I sighed. I hated waiting under normal circumstances, but add in my nervous energy and it was excruciating.

"We'll make it," Alec said, reading my mind.

"I have no patience for people just standing around. Look at them up there. It's like they're window shopping or something."

Alec looked at me. "Settle down there, Seattle Slew. We'll get there."

"Don't compare me to a horse," I warned. The nerves I was experiencing surprised me. I thought I would be excited and raring to go, not a bundle of nerves and ready to back out.

"When we get our race bibs, I'll be going up to the first corral. You'll be in the last corral since you've never raced before," he informed me. "Horses."

"What? What do you mean?" I asked, turning to him. "You're leaving me alone?"

"I told you that," he reminded me.

"No, you did not," I assured him. I couldn't remember him mentioning it before, but I couldn't swear that he hadn't.

"I did," he said calmly. "Corrals are set up by previous race times and you have no previous race times. Therefore, you will be in the last corral. We don't want you getting trampled by faster runners."

"I don't want to run by myself. I realize you'll run faster than I will, but I want you by my side when we start."

"You'll be fine, Allie," he said. "I promise. And if we do this often enough and if you run fast enough, one day you'll be in the big kids' corral just like me."

I breathed out hard. I loved this man, but some days he was difficult.

Chapter Two

ALEC WAS RIGHT. THERE were porta-potties all along the racecourse. I knew because, by mile twenty-one, I had made five stops. It seemed the race gels designed to keep my flagging energy up didn't agree with me. It didn't matter, though. I couldn't feel much of my body by the twenty-first-mile marker, anyway. My feet and legs were lumps of numbness and I was afraid if I stopped to wonder how they were still moving, I would fall flat on my face. I couldn't remember why I had thought running a marathon was a good idea.

I hadn't seen Alec since he had bragged about being in the first corral. I had also lost track of the scared-looking girl from the ladies room. For someone that looked terrified of what we were about to do, she could really move. I wondered if the scared look was all an act designed to make her opponents underestimate her so she could easily leave them in the dust.

As I trudged along, my eyes darted to the sidelines. There were volunteers holding out paper cups of Gatorade and water. I put my hand out and miraculously a cup of orange Gatorade appeared. I still hadn't figured out how that worked, but by my estimation, I had had at least thirty cups of the orange miracle fluid today.

I glanced at my watch and realized I had been at this for over four hours. I would not qualify for the US Olympic team at this rate, and with a time like that I would be stuck in the fourth corral forever.

Running a marathon was nothing like I had imagined. I thought I would run with a smile on my face and energy to spare. Sure, I knew I'd be tired when I got to the end, but at mile thirteen I had broken down in tears. I had run too fast at the beginning and when I realized I was only halfway done, I fell apart. Fortunately, a kind-hearted runner took hold of my hand and talked me through it. I never got her name, but she was an angel in green spandex.

At mile fifteen my cheeks and lips had chapped from the tears and the blowing breeze. I desperately wished I had thought to stow Chapstick somewhere on my person.

Thankfully the weather was good with the forecast saying seventy-six degrees. It was early yet, so it was still nice and cool. In spite of that my hair piled atop my head made me feel like my scalp was on fire. I had a lot of hair and it acted as an incubator for my scalp. By mile eighteen, I wished I had thought to shave my head before the race.

My feet pounded the pavement, and I swallowed. I had a serious case of cottonmouth in spite of the Gatorade and I hoped Alec didn't want to kiss me when I crossed the finish line. Was Alec already through? Probably. His long legs had most likely eaten up the miles in record time.

I breathed in deep and my lungs screamed in pain. Was that supposed to happen? I didn't know, but I hoped it wasn't anything permanent. Maybe forty-something was too old to run a first marathon. What had I been thinking?

A woman with pink hair was standing with a sign at the mile twenty-two marker. She held a yellow fluorescent sign that said, *Go Allie, Go! You can do it!*

Aw, I thought. Allie's so lucky to have someone to cheer her on. Then I realized my name was Allie and that woman with the sign was Lucy. I would have cried except I was pretty sure I didn't have any fluid left in my body. I forced my mouth into a smile and felt my lips crack. I waved at her as I passed. At least, I think I did. I'm pretty sure it looked more like a flail, though.

THE FINISH LINE WAS up ahead and I could make it if I could forget my legs were still attached to my body. They were a weird mixture of numb and throbbing pain. I pushed myself and smiled at the remaining people lined up along the finish line, waving and cheering. I flailed my hands again and tried to remember what Alec looked like. My brain was as exhausted as my body. Was he there waiting for me?

I pushed myself across the finish line and someone slammed into me, causing my forward motion to cease. I closed my eyes and felt my head spin. Why didn't people watch where they were going?

"Allie, Allie," I heard someone say. I wanted to open my eyes, but it didn't seem like it was worth the effort, so I let them stay shut. "Allie, are you okay?"

I smiled again. At least, I think that's what I was doing. I felt water being poured on my neck and head and my eyes flew open. "Hey! What are you doing?" I slurred and felt myself being turned over to lie on my back.

"Are you okay, Allie?" someone said. I squinted at the person holding my shoulders up off the ground. Alec. So that's what he looked like. I smiled. He held a plastic cup of water and was poised to pour it on my face.

"Hey. Did I make it?" I croaked.

He grinned. "You did. You made it across the finish line and then you fell. It kind of looked like your legs wobbled and gave out."

"I did?" I asked. I couldn't remember any of that, but I would take his word for it. "Time?"

He glanced up at the clock behind me. "Just under five hours."

I frowned. "I can't get into Boston with that time."

"No, you can't. But you did great. You finished your first marathon and a lot of people don't make it that far. I'm proud of you."

I nodded and closed my eyes.

"Let's get you up on your feet and get fluids in you. Did you hydrate along the course?" he asked.

I nodded.

"Allie, are you okay?" I heard a voice say.

I opened one eye and saw a pink-haired lady. The same one that was holding the sign. Lucy. I nodded. "I'm fine. How about you?"

Alec hoisted me to my feet, and he put my arm around his neck. "Let's get her something to drink."

"I'm fine, Allie, but I'm not sure about you," Lucy answered.

"I'm good. I finished," I assured her. I gripped Alec's neck as we walked.

Alec walked me across the fairgrounds and over to our booth. My feet screamed with each step and I wondered if I had worn all the skin off the bottom of them.

"I'm hungry," I said. As soon as it was out of my mouth, I felt a wave of nausea wash over me and I grimaced. "Never mind."

"Let's get some water and Gatorade into you," Alec said. Ed pulled out one of the folding chairs and Alec sat me down on it. "Lean against the chair back and try not to fall off."

"Got it," I said. My skin felt like it was on fire, but I felt cold at the same time. I needed sleep.

Alec was back quickly with a bottle of Gatorade, and twisted the lid off. He put the bottle to my cracked lips, and it was the most divine tasting liquid I had ever tasted. I drank and drank, forgetting to come up for air.

"You need to drink more often when you run," Alec said, kneeling beside my chair. "It's dangerous letting yourself go so long without fluids."

I nodded, taking the bottle from him, and drained it. "I love this stuff."

"I'll get her some more," Lucy volunteered and went in search of more of the delightful orange elixir.

"How do you feel?" Alec asked with a grin on his face.

"Like I've been run over by a steamroller. I'm pretty sure being steamrolled feels like this."

He nodded. "You get used to it."

"I don't want to get used to it. I want a cupcake. And not one of those tiny ones, either."

Alec nodded and chuckled. This wasn't funny. Why hadn't he told me I would feel like death after the race? My head felt enormous and my muscles quivered.

Ed handed me a cupcake, and I shoved it in my mouth whole. My mama would be disappointed, but I didn't care. The sweet delicious strawberry flavor was better than anything I had ever tasted. Who made this thing? Then I remembered I made it. Apparently, I knew a thing or two about how to make cupcakes.

"Here you go," Lucy said, handing me another bottle of Gatorade. She held two more in reserve and waited while I finished my cupcake.

"Why did we do this?" I asked Alec. "It makes no sense. We paid good money to torture ourselves."

He sat there and grinned at me and shook his head. "You did a great job. You should be proud."

I didn't feel like I did a great job. I felt like I had survived an ordeal. I would think twice, or maybe three times before attempting another marathon.

Chapter Three

I SAT ON THE CHAIR for at least forty-five minutes letting Alec tell me how awesome I was for finishing the marathon. I appreciated it, but I didn't feel awesome and I didn't feel like ever running again. Becoming a couch potato sounded attractive. It was much safer and less painful.

"It might be a good idea for you to take a walk," Alec suggested.

I narrowed my eyes at him. "I thought you loved me?"

He looked confused. "I do. What do you mean?"

"If you loved me, you'd let me sit here. For eternity, if need be."

"You need to walk around and get your muscles moving. You've already sat too long," he said.

I sighed and gave him my hand. "Help me up."

He put his arm around me and helped me get to my feet. That was when I bit my lower lip to keep from screaming. I hurt. Everywhere. What had I done to myself?

"Come on, you can do it," he encouraged.

"Fine. I want some strawberries. I'm starving," I said. And I was. My stomach felt like it had a hole in it.

"All right, let's go." He kept one arm around me and we meandered along the rows of booths. Across from ours was a strawberry salsa booth, and I wanted to take a look. Jars of strawberry salsa sat on the table, along with a bowl of tortilla chips to sample the salsas. Each jar had a fancy label on it boasting of being locally made. There were other flavors besides strawberry, and I thought I would try them all.

"Is the strawberry salsa good?" I asked the girl behind the booth.

"The best," she said, and pushed a bowl of tortilla chips along with a little plastic sample cup of salsa toward me. "We have mild, medium and spicy."

I took a chip and dipped it into the medium salsa and brought it to my mouth. "Oh, my gosh, that is so good!" I scooped up more salsa on another chip and shoved it in before I had swallowed the first.

Alec scooped salsa onto a chip, and ate it, nodding. "That is really good."

I thought the chilies in the salsa would overwhelm the strawberries but it somehow complemented them. I scooped up more salsa on a chip and popped the whole thing into my mouth. "So good," I said around the food in my mouth.

"We better buy a jar," Alec said, reaching for his wallet as I scooped another chip full of salsa into my mouth.

"Wow," I said and grabbed another plastic cup of salsa and scooped it up with a chip. I probably looked greedy, but I was starving and the salsa was a beautiful thing.

Alec smirked. "She seems to like it," he said to the girl and handed her the cash. "We'll take two jars. Medium and spicy."

"Great," she said and put two jars into a plastic bag for him.

I scooped up another chip full of salsa and Alec guided me away from the booth. "Save some for the other people," he whispered.

"No," I said around the chip and salsa in my mouth. My mother taught me not to talk with food in my mouth, but I was making an exception to the rule today. "You should get five jars. Maybe six. This stuff is great."

"We can come back for more if we really need it," he said. He put the plastic bag with the salsa over his arm and wrapped his other arm around me to keep me walking. "Let's see what we've got here."

The next booth had soaps and candles on the table. Along the back of the booth were strawberry plants and fancy labeled bottles of vitamins and supplements.

"What's all that?" I asked, pointing to the bottles in the back.

The man stepped up to the front of the booth and looked back over his shoulder to where I was pointing. "That's botanical heaven. I'm a botanist and I grow my own healing herbs. Western medicine is harmful to the human body, you know. Nature has given us all we need to stay healthy and smart people take advantage of those resources."

"Oh," I said, nodding. The guy was a little intense.

He stuck his hand out. "I'm Barnabas Smithfield. I own a little greenhouse and organic garden just outside of town. There's a shop on the property and I sell vitamins, herbs, and natural medicines." Barnabas had shoulder-length black hair, a black goatee and wore gold wire-framed glasses. He had an engaging smile and blue eyes that twinkled. I liked him immediately.

"Alec Blanchard," Alec said, shaking Barnabas's hand. "And this is Allie McSwain."

I stuck my hand out and shook Barnabas's hand. It surprised me that it was cold and clammy. It took all the control I could muster to keep from wiping my hand on my shirt.

"So what kind of herbs do you grow?" I asked, making conversation.

"I've got over three hundred types of plants. It's not only my hobby but also my livelihood. Your complexion could use some witch hazel. It will clear up those abrasions," he said, eyeing my red, dried-out face.

I narrowed my eyes at him. "I just ran a marathon. My complexion might not be quite as clear as it normally is." I was beginning to change my initial assessment of him. His mama obviously hadn't told him that a gentleman doesn't mention when a lady doesn't look her best.

"Oh, of course," Barnabas said. "But if you'd like to hasten the healing process, you can't go wrong with witch hazel."

I could sense Alec snickering silently beside me and I had to keep myself from looking at him or I would slug him in the arm.

"And you make soap?" Alec asked, looking at the array of bars on the table in front of us.

Barnabas nodded. "Goat's milk soap. In honor of the festival, I added strawberries, and then I added coconut oil for its medicinal properties. Coconut oil is very good for the complexion and the seeds in the strawberries act as exfoliates."

I nodded. It sounded good. "May I see a bar?"

He reached over and picked up a pink bar and handed it to me. "Go ahead. Smell it."

I put it up to my nose and inhaled. "Wow. That smells good. What else is in it?" The bar had a light pink and white swirl pattern. The strawberry seeds were easily seen on small chunks of strawberries throughout the bar.

"Almonds and honey. You could almost eat it," he said and chuckled. "Oh, but don't. It doesn't taste as good as it smells."

I smiled at him. "I'm loving the festival so far," I said. "Everyone's so creative with the items they're selling. I never knew there were so many things you could do with strawberries."

"Yes, it's delightful, isn't it? Of course, you have to watch out for the less scrupulous sellers," he said, looking down the row of booths.

"Oh?" I asked.

He nodded. "Yes. Some people think it's perfectly fine to steal ideas from others and make a profit from them."

I wasn't sure what he was talking about, but I wanted to see more of the festival. It was time to move on.

"I'd like some soap," I said to Alec. "And what about that?" I asked, pointing to a box of lip balm tubes on the side shelf of the booth.

"Lip balm. Honey and strawberries. All natural ingredients, just like the soap."

"I need two of those, too, please. My lips are chapped after that run," I said, licking my lips.

"Ring us up for a couple bars of soap and two lip balms," Alec said, taking his wallet out again.

"And something for the lady's skin?" Barnabas suggested. "I also have vitamin E oil with aloe for your skin. It helps with windburn."

I narrowed my eyes at him again. "I don't need anything for my skin besides the soap. Thanks."

"Very well," Barnabas said with a shrug. "Too bad you weren't here earlier. I made smoothies for the runners with all natural ingredients to help with recovery. They went like hotcakes though, and I'm sold out."

"That's a shame," I said. "I love smoothies."

"Remember, be careful of the other sellers. Especially the ones selling soaps and botanicals. They don't use all natural ingredients. Some have stolen my ideas, but they cut corners," he said, nodding his head.

"We sure will," I said with a tired smile. I didn't know what he had against the other sellers and I was too tired to care.

Alec paid for my loot and we walked on. My legs protested every step of the way, but I had to admit they were feeling looser from walking. Alec was right about me sitting for so long after the race. I needed to keep moving to loosen my muscles and joints.

We stopped in front of a booth with strawberry cookies on display and I was about to pick out a strawberry white chocolate chip cookie as big as my head when we heard a scream.

"She fainted! Someone call 911!" a voice screamed.

"Come on," Alec said. We headed toward a booth selling strawberry jam and fresh strawberries. A small crowd was gathering and Alec left me to see what was happening. I hobbled after him as best I could.

Alec jumped the front of the booth and kneeled down behind it. My legs protested as I forced myself to move faster. The front of the booth was already lined with people, but I nudged my way to the front and peered over the side.

A young woman with dark brown hair lay on her back on the ground. There was foam and pink stuff coming out of her mouth and her body jerked now and then. Alec was on the phone talking to the 911 operator while people stood around silently watching. When Alec had an ambulance on the way, he hit END and turned back to the girl.

"Aren't you going to give her CPR?" someone in the crowd asked.

"She's still breathing," Alec said without looking away from the girl. He placed his hand on the girl's neck, checking for a pulse.

He was silent a moment and without a word, he began CPR.

"Oh, no," someone said.

I bit my lower lip. The twitching made me wonder if she was having a seizure.

"Do you need me to do anything, Alec?" I asked.

He shook his head. "Not right now."

"Oh, poor thing," someone said.

"Is she going to be okay?" someone else asked.

"Allie, can you get us some privacy?" Alec asked, without stopping CPR.

"Let's give her some privacy, everyone," I said, waving my hands. People along the front of the booth glanced at me and took a step back. "Please everyone, if that was someone you loved, you'd want her to have privacy."

I kept waving them away and wished Lucy and Ed were there to help, but they were too far away. "Come on, everyone. Please move back."

A middle-aged man at the back stepped up and helped me back up the crowd. Some people wandered off, but most only backed up a little. It was the best we could do. I prayed the ambulance got here soon.

Chapter Four

ALEC SAT ON THE FOLDING chair with his head in his hands. I stood behind him and rubbed his shoulders. "You did all you could do."

"I know," he said without looking up.

I felt terrible for Alec. We both knew he had done all he could for the girl, but we both also knew he would blame himself for not being able to resuscitate her.

"I'm sorry, Alec," Lucy said.

"Thanks," Alec said, still not looking up.

"There wasn't anything else you could do," Ed said. "If anyone knew what to do to save her life, it was you."

"I know," Alec repeated. "I just can't stand that it happened to someone so young."

I looked up as a man in a suit approached. He had a crew cut, and he moved with an air of authority, very much like Alec moved when he was in charge and investigating a case. He stopped at the booth and looked at Alec, still with his head in his hands, and then at me. Finally, his eyes rested on Ed and Lucy.

"Excuse me, I'm Detective Calvin Black with the Sanford police department. I'd like to ask you folks a few questions."

Alec's head popped up. "Cal, I haven't seen you in years. What are you doing in this area?"

The detective's face broke out into a grin. "Alec Blanchard. I haven't seen you in what, ten years? How are you? I moved to this neck of the woods about eight years ago."

"I'm living over in Sandy Harbor. I'm here for the marathon and the Strawberry Festival. This is my girlfriend Allie McSwain, and these are our friends Lucy and Ed Gray."

"Pleased to meet you all," he said, nodding at the three of us. "Alec, were you the one that administered CPR?"

Alec nodded. "I did. But she didn't respond." His mouth formed a hard line.

The detective whipped out his notebook and pen. I thought detectives probably all bought their pens and notebooks at the same place. Detective Supplies 'R Us. Alec may have retired from the police force, but he still kept a supply of notebooks for his private investigation agency.

"Can you tell me what happened?" he asked.

"We were at a booth not far away from where the victim was and we heard someone scream that she had fallen. I ran over and saw her on the ground. She was still breathing when I checked her, so I dialed 911. I doubt it was over two minutes from the time she fell to when she stopped breathing and I began CPR."

Cal made notes and looked back at him. "Did you notice anything else?"

Alec shook his head. "Just that there was foam as well as a pink substance around her mouth, and her body was twitching a bit. A crowd gathered pretty quickly, but I didn't see anything unusual."

Cal made more notes, and then looked up at him. "If you think of anything, you'll call me, right?" he said and handed him a business card.

"You know it," Alec said, taking the card from him.

"So how's life been treating you? You still on the force?"

Alec shook his head. "No, I retired the end of last year and started a private investigation business. Not much goes on in Sandy Harbor, but I've gotten a little work from the police department. They've cut back on personnel and don't have a detective now, so they still ask me to work with them from time to time."

"That's a good deal. I heard Sam Bailey is chief of police there. I'd hate to work for him. He was always a little difficult, if you know what I mean."

"I did work for him and I did hate it," Alec said, with a smile. "Anything new with you?"

"Nope. Not really," Cal said. "Just putting my time in so I can retire in a few years."

Someone cried out, and we all turned to look toward the booth where we had found the girl. Alec jumped to his feet, and we all headed in that direction.

When we got to the booth, a young man was inside, walking back and forth with the back of his hand across his forehead. He was shirtless and wore a pair of white cutoffs. His medium length blond hair was sweat-damp around the edges and worry creased his forehead.

"What happened?" he cried to the blond woman near the booth.

The woman shrugged and whispered something, then glanced in Alec's direction.

"Excuse me," Cal said and introduced himself. "You knew the victim?"

"Yeah, she's my girlfriend. Where is she? Someone said Tessa fainted."

"She was transported to the hospital. Can you tell me where you've been?" Cal asked.

"What?" the man asked, looking puzzled. "I was looking at the other booths."

Cal wrote in his notebook. I wondered why the young man hadn't heard the earlier commotion and sirens. When Tessa had been put into the ambulance, I would have sworn the entire festival crowd had gathered near to watch.

"I need to go to her," he said. "What happened to her? Do you know?"

Cal shook his head. "She stopped breathing and Detective Blanchard here performed CPR on her. Can I get your name?"

He looked at Cal. "Rich McGinty. Why are you asking me these questions? I need to get to Tessa."

"Why don't we talk in private?" Calvin suggested.

"Why? What's going on?" Rich asked. His voice quivered as Calvin led him away toward the parking lot.

"Wow," I said. I felt like crying, but I didn't want to break down in front of all the people milling about.

"What about the booth?" Lucy asked, looking at the booth with jars of strawberry jam.

"I've been watching it since the ambulance took the young lady away," the blond woman at the booth next door said. "I'm sure someone will come to pack up her things at some point."

"That's a good idea," Alec said. "If someone doesn't come by, we can have Cal contact her family."

The woman nodded. "It's no problem."

I went back to my booth and sat down, people watching those that walked by. I couldn't believe the woman had died. She was just too young.

Ed and Lucy returned after a few minutes. We were all shaken by what had happened and we sat in silence. A few people stopped by for samples, but not many were buying my cupcakes.

I had only sold a dozen cupcakes by the end of the day, and it was a little disappointing. People were shaken by the girl's death and weren't in the mood to buy. I hoped the next day would be better. We had the booth for the whole week and a carnival would be in town for two days. I thought the carnival might lighten the mood of the festival.

Alec came back and handed me the bag of salsa and soaps he had bought for me. "You thought I lost these, didn't you?"

"It had crossed my mind," I said, taking the bags from him.

"I did misplace them for a bit," he admitted.

I smiled. "We aren't selling much." I didn't blame anyone for not being in the mood to buy. I wasn't in the mood to sell and I wondered if I should cancel for the rest of the festival.

"There's been a lot of excitement," he said. "People have other things on their minds."

"I know. It's so sad."

"It's a bad start to what's supposed to be a fun week," Lucy said, frowning.

I nodded. "I might be too tired to come down here tomorrow."

"Ed and I can handle it," Lucy said. "What we don't sell, Ed will finish up."

Ed had a cupcake halfway to his mouth, and he stopped with his mouth still open. "Hey. I'm just making sure they're fresh. Nothing wrong with that."

"Help yourself. I will have a lot left over," I said. "I guess I can hand them out before we get ready to leave. If I'm going to come back tomorrow I'll need to pick up more strawberries before we go." I was undecided about coming back. Part of me really wanted to, but the other part of me wanted to stay home in bed.

"What are you going to make for tomorrow?" Lucy asked.

I shrugged. "Maybe strawberry tarts. Speaking of tarts," I said when I spotted a familiar figure approaching.

A familiar looking petite woman with dark hair and black-framed glasses strode toward the booth. Her arms were crossed over her chest and she frowned at my cupcakes sitting on the table. I had put them under glass so people could see them. She stopped and looked me up and down, scowling.

"You foolish woman. You think these will sell?" she said in a thick French accent and motioned to my cupcakes.

"Suzanna. What are you doing here?" I sneered. The last person I expected to see at the festival was my newly acquired archrival.

"That's something I could ask you," she said. "You do not have even a basic grasp on baking. Why do you waste your time?"

Lucy gasped. "You mean little woman. I'd put Allie's cupcakes up against your whatever-it-is you make, any day. Allie is an expert baker."

Suzanna tossed her head back and laughed. "You two are something else. You know nothing of baking. You waste my time! And what is that pink hair for?" Suzanna narrowed her eyes at Lucy's hair and frowned.

Lucy gasped and scowled at her. "Duh! Strawberry Festival. People love my strawberry pink hair."

"You're the one that came over here," I pointed out to Suzanna. "What do you want?"

"I came to see what other people are selling. Just like everyone else. You obviously are not selling anything. If you get hungry, come and taste my strawberry crème cake. Oh, wait, on second thought. Don't. I banned you from eating my food." She laughed again and people turned to look in our direction.

I glanced at Alec sitting on the chair. His eyebrows furrowed as he watched Suzanna. I wondered when he would step in and tell the little creep to hit the road.

"Who is this?" he asked, turning to me.

"That little French tart from La Chemise," I said. "I told you about her. Can't you see how arrogant she is?"

He nodded. "Indeed I do."

Suzanna and I had had a run-in several months earlier. She had opened an authentic French restaurant in Sandy Harbor, stealing customers from Henry's Home Cooking Restaurant, and in turn, from me. I slipped in to buy some of her French desserts, just as research, you understand, and she confronted me, banning me from her restaurant. I'm still not sure who ratted me out and blew my cover, but if I ever find out, there will be trouble. Suzanna was a pompous little Frenchwoman and I couldn't stand her.

"La Chemise? I like that restaurant," Ed said, brightening.

"See? Even your friend likes my food. That's why he's chubby. He can't stay away from my food because it is the best!"

I gasped. "Ed isn't chubby. But if he was chubby, it would be because of my desserts, not yours!"

"Lucy, am I chubby?" Ed asked, frowning and looking at his wife.

"Hush, Ed," Lucy said. "You're perfect and I wouldn't change you for anything."

"What are you doing here, anyway?" I asked Suzanna. "No one will drive from Sanford to Sandy Harbor to go to your restaurant."

"Of course they will. I have people travel from all over the state to taste my cuisine."

The little imp looked so pleased with herself. The sad thing was, she had a reason to be. Her desserts were some of the best I had ever eaten. They might have been better than mine, and since she had moved to town and opened her restaurant, my business was suffering.

"Why don't you find someone else to torment and go darken their day?" Lucy suggested.

"Fine. I have no interest in any of you, anyway," she said and spun around and walked away.

I would like to say I made a snappy retort as she left, but I didn't. It had been a long hard day, and I was ready to go to the motel and go to bed.

Chapter Five

THE SHOWER I TOOK AT the motel was the best thing I have ever experienced. My muscles begged for more hot water, but when my skin turned pruney, I forced myself to get out. My muscles ached as I moved around the room and I wondered once again why I had put myself through the marathon. Next time, I would watch it on TV.

I got dressed, putting on a pair of jeans and a t-shirt. If Alec wanted fancy, he would be disappointed. I was exhausted. What I didn't understand was why wasn't Alec exhausted? Alec wanted to go out to eat, and all I wanted to do was go to bed. I'd have been fine with a taco from the drive-thru at this point.

When I was dressed, I sat on the edge of the bed and lay back. My eyes closed, and I was asleep before I knew it.

A sharp knock at the door woke me. I jumped and suppressed a scream. I sat up and stared at the door, trying to remember where I was.

The knock came again, and I forced myself to my feet. I peered through the peephole and then opened the door.

"Hey," I said. Alec was standing there with his hand poised to knock again.

"Hey," he said, stepping inside and giving me a kiss. "You look beautiful."

I snickered. "Right. I look like I was dragged behind a wagon pulled by six horses with their tails on fire. Can't we get McDonald's and go to bed?"

"Lucy and Ed want to eat out. We need to eat too, so let's go out," he said. "Ready?"

I nodded reluctantly, and let him lead me out of the room.

We chose a casual 1950s style diner, and I was glad. I wasn't wearing makeup, and I thought someone might think I was sick. In a casual diner I wouldn't have to pretend to be pretty.

"I want a cheeseburger. With fries. And a chocolate shake," I said and laid my menu on the table.

Alec looked at me.

"What? I burned a million calories today."

"I didn't say anything," Alec murmured. "Although your nutrition is questionable these days. If you would eat more fresh greens, you might not feel as bad as you do now."

I elbowed him, and stuck my tongue out. Alec would never reform my eating habits and he knew it.

The waitress took our orders, and I leaned back in the booth. I was sitting next to the wall, so I laid my head against it and closed my eyes.

"Hello, fancy meeting you all here," I heard a voice say.

My eyes popped open, and I sat up. Had I dozed off? I had the feeling a lot of time had somehow passed in the few moments I had my eyes closed. Cal stood in front of our table.

"What's up, Cal?" Alec asked him.

"It looks like foul play may be involved in the death of the young woman at the festival. I know you saw she was foaming at the mouth, but she also had blisters in her mouth and down her throat."

"Oh no," I said. "How awful."

"Do they have any idea what might have happened to her?" Lucy asked.

He shook his head. "No, they haven't done the autopsy, but when they do, they'll have to send samples to toxicology. On the plus side, I think we might get the reports back sooner than we normally would."

"Why is that?" Alec asked, picking up his glass of water.

"The woman's name was Tessa Brady. She's the mayor's daughter."

"And the mayor's office is putting pressure on the police department to get answers," Alec said.

Cal nodded. "That they are."

"If you need any help on the case, I'll be glad to do what I can. We're staying at a motel tonight, and going home the remaining days. But Sandy Harbor isn't far away," Alec offered.

Cal nodded. "I appreciate that and I may take you up on that offer. I had a question for Allie though." He looked at me with a smile.

"What? A question?" My mind was still foggy with sleep.

He nodded. "There was something pink on Tessa's face and residue in her mouth. It looks exactly like the frosting on those strawberry cupcakes you made."

I gasped. "What do you mean? What are you saying?"

Cal shrugged. "We need to wait for the toxicology reports, but it does look like the frosting on those cupcakes."

"Cal, I assure you, Allie is not responsible for the girl's death," Alec said.

"I'm not saying she is. I'm just pointing it out and I'm wondering if you remember seeing her come to your booth to buy cupcakes?" he asked.

I shook my head. "I ran the marathon and I've been pretty worn out ever since. I can't remember much of anything. But there had to be someone else selling something pink she might have eaten. It's the Strawberry Festival, after all."

"Absolutely true," he said, nodding. "I'm not saying anything else. I'm just trying to piece things together. If we can get a timeline on her, it might tell us something important and if she was at your booth, I'd like to know."

"I don't remember seeing her either," Alec offered. "We both ran the race. Allie was running until around an hour before we found the girl."

Cal looked at Lucy and Ed. "Do either of you remember her?"

"I didn't get a look at her," Lucy said. "Maybe if you had a picture of her, I might remember."

"I have one here," he said, removing a picture from his notebook. He handed it to Lucy, and she looked it over.

The girl was young and pretty. I didn't think she could be much over twenty-one. It made me sad to think someone so young had died before getting a chance to live her life.

Lucy studied the picture, and shook her head. "I don't remember her."

Ed shook his head after looking at it. "Me either."

Lucy handed the picture back and Cal put it into his notebook. "If any of you can think of anything else, you'll let me know, right?"

"We certainly will," Alec said. "Was her boyfriend able to give you any information?"

"Not a lot. He was having a hard time processing that she had died, but I'm on my way over to talk to him again. I just stopped in to get something to carry out for dinner."

"What kind of girl was she?" I asked him. "Being the mayor's daughter, I would think she was pretty straitlaced, but you never know."

"You never know how people live in their private lives," Alec agreed. "I'm sure you've seen that before." He looked at Cal when he said that last part.

"I have," Cal agreed. "It's hard to say what kind of person Tessa was at this point. I'll interview the Mayor and his family tomorrow to find out more about Tessa. Hopefully they can shed some light on things. Well, I'll let you enjoy your dinner."

The waitress came up behind Cal with a tray carrying our food and he went to the front register to place his order.

The waitress put our food on the table and left. I looked at Alec.

"What do you think it means? Why would he think it's my cupcake on her face?" I asked. "Do I seem suspicious?"

Alec shrugged. "You gave him cupcakes to take home to his family. I'm sure it was on his mind when the hospital said there was something pink on her face and in her mouth."

It was true. I hadn't sold many cupcakes and when he walked by my booth on his way out of the festival, I gave him a dozen cupcakes to take home to his family. That was the last time I'd be nice to him.

"Well, my cupcakes did not kill her," I insisted. "I am not a killer."

"Of course you're not," Alec said with a chuckle. "Don't jump to conclusions."

"You have to admit it's kind of scary," Lucy said, picking up her roast beef sandwich. "When a detective tells you your food was on the lips of someone that may have died from poisoning, it makes you wonder if you might be a suspect."

"Don't jump to conclusions," Alec repeated. "Tessa Brady could have had a seizure or an aneurysm or something of that nature. We won't know until the police get the toxicology reports back."

I didn't like it. It felt like Cal was the one jumping to conclusions. I was not the murdering kind, and I didn't even know Tessa Brady. I hoped she had had an allergic reaction to something. I also hoped the police figured out what killed her as soon as possible.

Chapter Six

"I WANT SOME OF THOSE," I said pointing to a display of chocolate dipped strawberries. "Please." Alec and I were wandering around the festival booths, hoping we could find more information about Tessa Brady's death. Someone had to have seen or know something. We still didn't know for sure if it was murder, but something deep down told me it was. I was getting a sense for this kind of thing. Call it intuition, or call it a good guess, but a healthy young woman does not suddenly drop dead.

"Let's get you some chocolate dipped strawberries then," Alec said, stepping up to the booth. The young woman running the booth was waiting on another customer, so we waited our turn.

"Oh, look. She has strawberry truffles," I said, reading the sign in front of the candy display. It was 10:00, and the festival had just opened. It was still chilly with low cloud cover, but I wondered how the woman would keep the candy from melting once the sun came out.

"How are you feeling after your little run yesterday?" Alec asked me.

"I still feel like a steamroller ran over me," I replied. "My legs feel like they weigh three hundred pounds apiece and it was not a little run. It was a great big, exhausting run."

Alec smirked. He was a smirker, that one.

"You get used to it. Or at the very least, you recover from it."

"I hope it's a quick recovery then. I could use it," I said as the other customer left with her candy. The young woman behind the booth turned to us and smiled.

"Hi, what can I help you folks with?" She looked to be in her late twenties or early thirties and had straight medium brown hair and the whitest teeth I've ever seen.

"The lady would like some chocolate dipped strawberries and some strawberry truffles," Alec said.

"Which kind of chocolate? Milk, white or dark?" she asked me with that brilliant smile.

"All three," I said. "Make it two of each. They all look so delicious, I can't decide on just one." I was starving. I figured it must have been from all the running I did the day before. I hoped the hunger went away before I gained ten pounds from the extra eating I was doing to get rid of the extra hunger.

"You got it," she said and picked up a small white bag to put the strawberries in.

"It's sad what happened to that girl yesterday," I said, making small talk.

"Oh, I know. I was talking to that girl earlier in the day. Did you hear what happened to her? Is she going to be okay?" the woman asked, turning back toward me.

I shook my head. "Sadly, no. She passed away."

The woman gasped and looked at me wide-eyed. "How terrible! Do they know what happened to her?"

"They have to do an autopsy and run some tests," Alec answered. "It's hard to believe someone so young would die suddenly like that."

"You said you spoke to her," I said. "Did you know her at all?"

She shook her head and put another strawberry in the paper bag. "No. When I was setting up my booth, she came over and asked if I had some tape. She had some signs to put up. I loaned her the tape, and we talked about the weather, the strawberries, but not much else. Poor thing. She looked like a healthy young woman. Why did she die?"

"It's too early to know," Alec said.

"How sad," she said. "I saw her a little later, walking from booth to booth. She stopped to chat with different people."

"It is sad," I agreed. "I feel bad for her and her family."

"What a tragedy. I'll go over to her booth and pay my respects to the people there. I don't know if they were family to her or not."

I nodded. "We're headed over there now."

Alec paid for my goodies, and we moved on down the row of booths. I looked longingly at the strawberry salsa booth as we passed and took a bite of a white chocolate dipped strawberry.

"Mm," I said. "I don't know how they grow these strawberries to be so sweet. I swear, these aren't like any strawberries around Sandy Harbor."

"They are good," Alec said. "Let's stop in at this booth."

I looked at the one Alec nodded at and we went to stand in front of it. The booth had rustic looking soaps and candles. Vanilla and strawberry scents hung in the air around the booth, and I inhaled. I remembered what Barnabas had said about being wary of other vendors selling soaps and I wondered if he meant this one.

"Yum," I said.

The young woman behind the booth chuckled. "That's what everyone says."

"It smells delicious," I said, looking over the candles. "Is it made of real beeswax?" I pointed at a large round candle with a honeycomb beeswax look.

She nodded. "Yes it is. I love these. I added cinnamon to that one. You can smell the cinnamon and the honey in them when they burn. They're all natural, so no chemicals are released into the air. Our soaps are all natural, too." She looked to be in her early twenties with blond hair, blue eyes with peaches and cream skin. She was a real cute girl that I thought must have been on her high school cheerleading team.

She said the soaps and candles were made from all natural ingredients and I wondered if Barnabas was wrong about the artificial ingredients or if he was just jealous of someone else selling soaps.

"They're nice to look at, too," Alec said, picking up a white and pink swirled candle with pieces of cut-up strawberry.

"Isn't it a tragedy what happened to that woman yesterday?" I asked her and picked up the honey cinnamon candle, brought it to my nose, and inhaled.

"Who, Tessa?" she snarled. Her face went from cute cheerleader to scary witch in about two seconds.

"Oh, did you know her?" I asked, turning the candle over in my hands. I wanted this candle, even though it didn't have strawberries in it.

She snorted. "I went to school with her. Let's just say she wasn't the nicest person. I wouldn't wish anything terrible on her, but I don't feel sorry for her, either."

Ah, cheerleader rivalry. A tale as old as time.

"Yes, but she died," I said, watching her face.

Her eyes went wide. "She did? I hadn't heard that. Well, that's a shame. A real shame." She nodded her head and looked away.

She didn't sound terribly sad for Tessa, but she did sound surprised.

"Yes, it's tragic. She looked so young and fit. You wouldn't expect someone like her to die suddenly," I said, glancing at Alec. "I can't imagine what happened to her."

The woman looked at Alec. "Aren't you the one that did CPR on her?"

Alec nodded. "I did. I'm trained in CPR, but unfortunately, there wasn't much I could do for her."

If she had been close enough to recognize Alec as the person who gave Tessa CPR, I thought she might have gathered around the booth with the onlookers and watched as Tessa's life slipped away, but she acted surprised to find out she had died. She also had something against Tessa. My intuition was twitching.

"Were you and Tessa close in school?" I asked. "I'm sorry, I didn't get your name?" I wanted to keep her talking. Maybe she would slip up and tell us something important.

Her face clouded over. "Tracie Jefferson. Tessa and I were best friends when we were younger. But then Tessa stole my boyfriend in high school. I guess you could say we were anything but close after that. It's not like I held a grudge, though. Hey, if Rich wanted to be with that—Tessa, it wasn't my business. I've got better things to do with my time than pine over him."

"Rich?" I asked. "The same Rich that was selling strawberry jam with her?"

"Yeah, the one and only," she said. "They broke up after dating a few months in high school and then got back together sometime last year. I don't keep track of those things, though. Rich never could make up his mind about what he wanted."

I nodded. "It's hard to know what men want sometimes."

"You can say that again. He played us both, but Tessa couldn't see it. She wouldn't see it. She was one of those desperate girls that chase after a guy long past the point when the guy shows he isn't interested. Then she was dumb enough to get back together with him after he dumped her. Idiot."

"That's a shame," I said. "There's no point in chasing someone that doesn't want you. It's a lack of self-esteem."

Tracie looked down at the candle in her hands. "That's what it is," she said, nodding.

I wondered if Tracie was the one with the self-esteem issue, and not Tessa. She was a beautiful girl and had no reason to feel that way, but you never could tell with some people.

"It's still a tragedy, any way you look at it. The poor thing died before she had a chance to live her life," I said.

She nodded, and another customer stepped up to the booth, asking questions about the candles.

"I want this candle," I said to Alec. "I forgot my purse at the booth, though."

Alec smirked. "How inconvenient," he said.

"What do you think about what she said?" I whispered while Tracie helped the other customer.

"I don't know. We'll make a note of it and keep it in mind."

We looked over the rest of the soaps and candles. I picked out a smaller candle and three bars of strawberry coconut soap. We waited while the young woman finished with the other customer and then Alec paid for my purchases.

Chapter Seven

WE HAD SPENT THE MORNING of day two walking all over the festival and I had spent a lot of Alec's money by the time we finished. Have I said how much I love this guy? He never complains about a thing. He's a real keeper.

We stopped back by the booth to check in on Lucy and Ed. My daughter Jennifer was sitting on a folding chair with her feet up on the edge of the booth.

"Hey, lazy," I said, pushing her sneaker-clad foot off the side of the booth.

"Hey. Not lazy. I made strawberry cream pies until late last night for you."

I smiled. "Okay, not lazy, but it's bad for business for you to have your feet on the edge of the booth. People might think those feet came in contact with the pies. And thank you for making the pies for me."

Jennifer was right. She had made the pies and strawberry cookies we were selling today. She had also made two dozen more strawberry cupcakes, and she was just about as good a baker as I was. I had taught her everything she knew. Jennifer was on summer break from college and I was glad. I needed her help.

"Got it. What's this I hear about a girl dying yesterday?" she asked, eyeing me.

"Yeah, it's sad. Alec gave her CPR, but she didn't make it. No word on the cause yet," I said, lifting the lid on a pie box. They smelled heavenly.

"She just dropped dead?" she asked with a horrified look. "How old was she?"

"Kind of. I'd guess she was in her early twenties. Someone screamed, and we went over to see what was happening and she stopped breathing."

"It's sad," Alec said, sitting on the edge of the booth.

We looked up at an approaching figure. Detective Calvin Black. I returned his smile and nudged Alec.

"Good morning, all," Cal said and nodded at me.

"Good morning, Cal," Alec said. "Anything new?"

"Well, I told you they would get right on this case due to Tessa being the mayor's daughter. It appears she died of asphyxiation," he said with a sigh.

"Asphyxiation?" Alec asked.

Cal nodded and leaned in close to whisper. "Her windpipe closed off. The Medical Examiner thinks she ingested something she was either allergic to or was poisonous. It's too early to tell, but off the record, things look suspicious."

"Maybe she was allergic to strawberries?" I suggested. "I've heard some people have allergies to strawberries and the reaction can be extreme."

"Not likely," Cal said, turning to me. "Her parents said she has no known allergies, and she eats strawberries all the time. Plus, she was in the middle of a strawberry festival. I don't think someone with a severe strawberry allergy would hang out around this many strawberries. And the pink frosting is still suspicious."

"You're not being serious, right? I mean, it's a coincidence she ate one of my cupcakes right before she died," I said, frowning at him. "Right?"

He shrugged. "We need to look at everything, and that's the most obvious thing right now. There was half of an uneaten cupcake in her booth that we sent over to toxicology to examine. We've asked them to put a rush on it."

I looked at Alec. "Tell him I am not a murderer. I didn't even know the girl. Why would I kill her?" I could feel the adrenaline rushing through my body and I wanted to tell this Calvin Black a thing or two.

"Now, Allie, calm down. Cal's just following procedure," Alec said, putting his hand on mine.

"You're taking his side?" I exclaimed. "What are you thinking?"

"I am not taking his side," Alec said, and then he turned to Cal. "Cal, I assure you that Allie isn't a murderer. She has never murdered anyone in her life, but right now she might be thinking about murdering me."

"Oh, thanks, Alec. You're making things better," I said, sticking my lower lip out. He was treading on thin ice.

Cal had a smirk on his face. "I completely understand. I'm not making accusations. I'm just telling you how things stand right now. The investigation has just gotten started and there's a lot we still need to look at."

"See?" Alec said, turning to me. "Everything is fine."

"And the thing is," Ed said from his corner of the booth, "Lucy was the one selling cupcakes yesterday. Allie was running the marathon so she couldn't have done it. Unless she poisoned a cupcake and then made sure Lucy sold it to the victim."

We all turned and looked at him. What on earth was he thinking?

"Ed. Shut up," Lucy said, crossing her arms over her chest.

"What?" he said and shrugged his shoulders. "We need to look at this thing logically."

"Seriously, Ed. Shut up," I said. "Neither Lucy nor I are murderers. We don't have a motive, regardless of what the girl ate. Got it?"

Ed nodded and fixed his eyes on a box of cookies on the table near him.

"I hope you both look good in stripes," Jennifer said.

"Jennifer, stop it," I warned.

I looked up and Alec and Cal were smiling.

"Stop it. Both of you. I don't think it's funny. Neither Lucy nor I had anything to do with a murder," I said, putting my hands on my hips. "You need to get out there and find the real killer."

They may have been enjoying the moment, but I was about to blow my top. If my legs hadn't felt like lead, I would have gone for a run to blow off steam.

"We still aren't positive it's a murder yet," Cal reminded me. "I've got to do interviews and we've got to wait on toxicology."

"I've talked to a couple of people," Alec said, pulling his notebook out of his pocket. "Not much yet, but we talked to an ex-friend of the victim. The relationship ended badly, and she didn't know anything about Tessa's death, of course."

"Got it," Cal said, taking a look at Alec's notebook. He whipped out his own and copied Alec's notes to it. "I appreciate your help, Alec. This is great."

Alec nodded. "You got it. Let me know if you need anything else."

"I sure will," Cal said. "I'm going to scout around and do some investigating of my own. I'll talk to you all later."

When he was out of earshot, I looked at Alec. "I really need you to stay on my side."

Alec put his hands up. "Sorry, I was just teasing you. Everything will be fine, you'll see. Cal needs to check out every possibility, but he's a good detective and he'll find the real killer."

"Fine," I pouted. I didn't like being looked at suspiciously and I hoped Cal did find the real killer.

Later, Alec and I took another walk and talked to people running booths. Alec made notes in his trusty notebook, but few people had seen much or even knew who Tessa was. We were a little disappointed with the results of our investigation.

Our last stop was the booth where Tessa and her boyfriend had been selling strawberry jam. A woman that looked a little older than Tessa sat on a folding chair, looking sad.

"Hi," I said. "I don't mean to intrude, but we wanted to express our condolences. We're so sorry about Tessa."

The woman looked up at me with tears in her eyes. "Thank you. Tessa was my cousin Rich's girlfriend. I just can't believe this."

"We're very sorry," Alec said. "I'm Alec Blanchard and this is Allie McSwain. I'm a private investigator and the police have asked me to help with the investigation into Tessa's death."

"Alec gave Tessa CPR," I said, nodding at Alec.

"Thank you for trying to save her," she said, entwining her fingers together. "It all seems like a bad dream. I can't believe this."

I nodded. "She was so young and looked like she was in good health. Did she have any health problems?"

She shook her head. "No. I mean, she really was in good health. She had planned on running the marathon, but a few weeks ago she pulled a muscle in her leg and it was slow in healing, so she decided not to run. She's always been a runner, though. Runners are healthy, right?"

I nodded. "I'm a runner and I rarely even get a winter cold."

"It's a shame," Alec said. "She never complained of not feeling well?"

She shook her head. "She took lots of vitamins and got plenty of sleep. She was almost obsessive with her health. She had a chance to try out for the Olympics this summer. It was her dream. I think she could have made it."

"Wow," I said. "She must have been an excellent athlete."

"Do the police think someone hurt her?" she asked Alec.

"I think everything's up in the air until they get test results back. They just want to make sure they know as much of what happened as possible," Alec said.

She nodded. "I see. I hope they get it figured out quickly. If someone did something to hurt her, then we need justice." Her mouth made a hard line and anger crept into her eyes.

"Can I get your name?" Alec asked.

"Susan Goode."

Alec made another note in his notebook. "We appreciate your time and if you remember anything else that may be of help, will you call me?" He whipped out a business card and handed it to her.

She nodded. "I will. I promise."

"Thank you, Susan," I said as we headed back to our booth.

"Wow. Trying out for the Olympics. Tessa must have been in excellent health," I said when we were out of earshot of Susan.

"I'll say. It's looking more and more like foul play. Sounds like someone might have had a grudge against Tessa," Alec said.

Chapter Eight

"STRAWBERRY TARTS. THAT's how I do the festival," I announced, holding up a box of the delectable little red jewels.

Alec peered into the open box I held up for his inspection. "Those look wonderful. I may need to sample them. You know, to make sure they pass inspection."

I gasped. "What are you saying, sir? Do you think my tarts might not pass inspection?"

He grinned. "There's a rumor going round that you may bake with a little extra flair. A poisonous flair."

"Alec!" I hissed. "Don't say that!" I glanced over my shoulder and saw an elderly woman eyeing us. I turned to her. "Good morning, Ma'am. It's a lovely day for a festival, isn't it?"

She snorted and walked on. I turned on Alec, glaring at him.

"She didn't hear me," he assured me with that wicked grin of his. "I swear. She just wasn't in the mood for strawberry tarts. With a special ingredient."

"Watch it, buddy." I put the box on the table and looked over at Lucy. "Some people."

"I love your strawberry tarts, Allie. I would never say they were poisonous," she said, leaning back in the folding chair. "Alec must not want any tarts."

"Okay, can we all please stop saying the 'P' word? Seriously? This isn't helping business," I warned.

I couldn't bake in a hotel room, so we had driven home the night before. I had stayed up late and finished my baking. Hopping into bed for a good night's sleep had been heavenly. I was regretting signing up for the entire week of the festival. We still had four more days to go, and I was exhausted. My legs felt like wood and all I wanted to do was take a nap for a day and a half.

Thank goodness my daughter Jennifer was holding down the fort at home and doing the baking for Henry's Home Cooking Restaurant. I didn't want to let Cynthia Hoffer down. Cynthia had been a dream to work with and I liked our little arrangement. All I had to do was come up with recipes for delectable baked goods, do the baking, and then drop them off at her restaurant. She handled the selling part and took a tidy little commission off the top.

Unfortunately, shortly after I started selling baked goods at Henry's, a new French restaurant had opened its doors, and the first two months had been disappointing for my new business. Authentic French desserts were a novelty in Sandy Harbor and people had flocked to the restaurant, leaving Henry's in the lurch. But things picked up a bit once I became more active with my baking blog. All in all, it had been a satisfying career change from blogging about grief.

"I'm hungry," Ed said as I set the tarts out on the booth table.

The tarts were covered in plastic wrap to keep flying critters off them and they looked sweet and pretty.

"We need to save some of them to sell," I pointed out and stowed the empty box under the table. "But I suppose we can share one or two of them."

I had made both petite tarts and larger ones so my customers would have a variety to choose from.

"I don't think I'll ever get tired of strawberries," Lucy said, helping herself to some of the fresh berries Alec had picked up for us.

"Me either. And look at this," I said, holding up a loaf of strawberry bread. "Sour cream strawberry loaf."

"Oh," Lucy said, eyeing the loaf of bread as I set it on the table. "My, my."

I pulled back the plastic wrap on the loaf and cut it into thin slices and then cut those into thirds. Samples always drew the crowds in. I had a glass-covered plate that I arranged the slices on and placed the lid on the plate.

"Now all we need to do is wait for the customers," I announced, pulling out two sizes of plastic-wrapped strawberry loaves and setting those next to the tarts. There was a small size for the petite appetite and larger for, well, the larger appetite. It all smelled heavenly, and I was ready to dive into my own baked goods.

A young couple walked up to the booth and eyed my offerings. Then they looked at me and the woman leaned over and whispered something to the man.

"Would you like a sample?" I asked, reaching toward the sample plate.

The woman leaned in close to the man and whispered again, and they walked off without a word. I looked over at Alec.

He shrugged.

"What was that about?" Lucy asked, picking up another berry.

"I don't know. Maybe they don't like strawberry loaf," I said. "Pity for them, because I happen to know how tasty it is."

I pulled out another folding chair and sat down. My feet still hurt, and I needed to give them a rest. I would have to think things over before agreeing to another marathon. Knowing it would be hard and actually experiencing how hard it was were two very different things.

"Uh oh," Lucy said.

I looked at her and then looked in the direction she had nodded.

Suzanna. I groaned.

She strode up to my booth and stopped, putting her hands on her hips. She glared at me, then looked down at my sample plate and the tarts.

"What is this?" she said, motioning toward my baked goods with her hand.

"Strawberry tarts and strawberry sour cream loaf," I said as politely as I could manage. I wasn't sure why she always had such an attitude with me. Sure, Lucy and I had sampled her desserts, hoping to come up with better recipes, but so what? It's not like we stole them. We paid for them fair and square.

She snorted. "It figures you would come up with something so plain and drab. Plain and drab desserts for a plain and drab woman." She gave me an evil smile when she said it.

I gasped. "You are the meanest little woman I have ever met," I declared. "Why do you have to be so—so mean?"

She snorted again. She was good at snorting so I guess she thought she ought to make use of it.

"You have no imagination. Why is that all you came up with? Why could you not come up with something more creative?"

"Well, what did you come up with?" I asked defensively. I glanced at my strawberry loaf and tarts. They weren't plain. They were tasty. And well, they smelled good, too.

"White chocolate spun around a strawberry napoleon and strawberry Fraisier." Her hands were still on her hips and she had a smile I wanted to wipe right off her pixie face in a not too gentle way.

"Well," I said, trying to come up with a classy retort. "That's nice. But really, sometimes people just want dessert that's tasty and—and," I trailed off. So much for a classy retort.

Alec sighed. "It's dessert. Dessert doesn't have to do back flips to please people."

I smiled at him. My hero.

Suzanna shrugged. "That's okay. Plain people need dessert, too, I suppose."

I could feel the anger rising inside of me. Why didn't that little woman find something else to do with herself besides torment me?

"Suzanna, don't you have something else to do with your time?" I asked her.

She chuckled. "I'm sorry. I've been unkind. I did not mean to be. Please accept my apology."

The look on her face said she wasn't the least bit sorry.

"Fine. I accept," I said. I could fake it if it got her out of my hair.

"Well, since you have nothing else to offer, I suppose I will go back to my booth. I've had so many customers this morning. How many have you had?"

I bit my lower lip. Darn her for asking. "A lot," I lied.

She looked at me skeptically. "A lot? Like, five? Ten? Twenty?"

I shrugged. "We don't keep track of that kind of thing. That would be bragging and my mama taught me not to brag." There. That would take care of her. I was certain her mama never taught her any sort of manners.

"I see. Then let me guess. Zero. It's zero, isn't it?" she asked with a smirk.

I clenched my teeth together. I relaxed them and smiled at her. "To tell you the truth, we just got here and got unpacked. I know we will see scads of customers any minute now. Why don't you run along and tend to your booth now?"

"All right. I've got a lot to do anyway," she said. "But if you need any help, let me know, okay?"

I looked at her. "Really?" It was unlike her to be kind to me.

"No," she said and laughed as she walked away.

"That woman!" I said, clenching my fists.

"Don't let her get to you, honey," Lucy said, patting my shoulder. "She's just a mean little woman. Your mama and your grandmama taught you better."

"That's right, they did," I said, nodding my head. I wished either of them were here right now. They'd give Suzanna what for and teach her some manners.

Chapter Nine

DAY FOUR WAS JUST AS lovely as the three before it. The sun was out, but the clouds made for a cool day. Strawberry apple muffins and strawberry cream cakes were the stars of the day. I cut up some muffins into bite-sized chunks and put them on the glass-covered sample plate.

"There. That should do it," I announced, putting my hands on my hips and looking at the displayed cakes and muffins. "What do you think?"

"Looks great," Lucy said and yawned.

"I know these early mornings are hard. You don't know how much I appreciate your help. And Ed's."

"Yeah, but the lazy lout stayed in bed this morning," Lucy said, stretching. "I'll tell him you paid me a hundred bucks for sitting with you today, and he missed out."

I chuckled. "You do that. I don't think he'll care much, though." Ed was the kind of guy that did what he wanted and not even money could persuade him to do something he didn't want to do.

I sat on the other folding chair and watched the people walk by. Sales for the previous three days had been disappointing. I'd gone home with an awful lot of what I had brought. It didn't make sense. The crowds were good and lots of people stopped by and looked at what I had brought to sell. A few tried the samples, but not many bought my desserts. Most people simply looked at me and moved on. Some whispered and looked at me pointedly before moving on and that was what was getting to me.

"Have you thought about why we aren't selling much?" Lucy asked as we watched people walk by.

I shrugged. "I've thought about it. I just don't know what that reason is."

I looked up just in time to see Calvin Black approaching, and I groaned. Alec may have considered him a friend, but he was a questionable friend as far as I was concerned.

"Where's Alec?" Lucy whispered.

"He went to check out the other booths again," I whispered back.

"Ladies, how are you doing this fine morning?" Calvin asked. He looked entirely too happy to see us and I didn't like it.

"We're doing just fine," I answered. "How's the investigation going?"

"That's what I've come to talk to you about." He grinned and it was a disturbing grin, to say the least. What was it about this guy that bugged me so much?

"Oh? What did you want to talk about?" I asked, trying to sound chipper.

"We've determined the pink substance on Tessa Brady's face is, in fact, strawberry frosting. Can you tell me, have you visited Sanford before the Strawberry Festival began?"

"What? What do you mean, have I visited Sanford before the Strawberry Festival?" I asked him. I didn't like this line of questioning and I wished Alec were here.

"I mean, have you been in the area before? Have you been to Sanford?" he repeated.

I sighed. "As a matter of fact, yes. I've come to the Strawberry Festival several times, but I think the last time was about ten years ago. I really couldn't give you an exact number, to be perfectly honest. And I am being perfectly honest."

Calvin whipped out his notebook and wrote something down. It took all the self-control I could muster to keep from sighing loudly. If Calvin Black thought I had something to do with Tessa's murder, he was sadly mistaken.

"And Lucy? What about you?"

Lucy's eyes went wide, and she looked at me. I shrugged. Calvin was wasting his time, and I needed to talk to Alec about it. Maybe he could get his zealous friend to back off.

"I—I, well, I suppose I've come to the festival a few times over the years," she said, looking at Calvin and smiling. "I don't remember how many times, though."

Calvin scribbled in his notebook again and I rolled my eyes at Lucy.

I saw Alec approaching over Cal's shoulder and relief swept over me. Alec would put an end to this foolishness.

"Hey, everyone," Alec said as he came to stand beside Calvin. "How are you, Cal?"

Calvin smiled at him. "I'm great. I just stopped by to ask the ladies a few questions."

"Oh?" Alec asked, and his face became serious. "What kind of questions?"

Cal shrugged. "Just wondering how often Allie and Lucy have been to Sanford. Before the festival began, I mean."

"Oh, come on Cal. I can assure you that Allie and Lucy are not killers. Have you even determined what the substance was in the victim's mouth? Did it really kill her? She could have eaten something innocuous that caused an allergic reaction in her."

Calvin looked down at the ground, then back at Alec and closed his notebook. "To be honest, we don't know what the substance is, and you are correct. She might have had an allergic reaction to something she ate. We know there was strawberry frosting in her mouth and on her face. As I've stated before, the mayor's office is breathing down our necks and we need answers. I decided to get information up front and cut down on the time I need to spend investigating after we get toxicology reports back." He smiled at Alec.

That Cal was a smug customer. I couldn't imagine Alec being friends with him. He made my skin crawl, and I hoped I wouldn't be seeing a lot of him while the festival ran.

"Or you're wasting your time," Alec pointed out. "If she died of some illness or allergic reaction."

"Humor me," Cal said. "Or I can insist we go downtown."

Alec motioned to me to answer Calvin's questions.

"What do you want?" I asked Calvin. I was done being polite. "I've been to the festival several times, and I didn't know Tessa Brady. I had no beef with her. But, she does have an ex-friend running around here that is, after all, an ex. Not to mention a boyfriend. Maybe you should spend some of your time interviewing them?"

"Yes, I'm aware of them and I'll be questioning them further," he said, making notes. "How about you, Lucy?"

"Like I said, I've been to Sanford a few times. I don't know how many, though. I didn't know the victim or anyone in her family." Lucy smiled at him and waited. We both felt more confident with Alec standing close by.

Cal finished his notes. "Do you recall the victim buying a cupcake from you? Allie said she was running the marathon, so I'm assuming you or your husband sold her the cupcake?"

Lucy shrugged. "I told you I didn't recognize her. She may have looked vaguely familiar, but I can't say for sure. I told you all of this before. We had lots of people stop by for samples and we sold regular sized cupcakes. Sometimes there were four or five people stopping by at a time and to be truthful, I didn't pay attention."

Cal eyed her and then nodded. "I understand. I can see where that might happen. There have been lots of people here at the festival."

"Lots," I agreed.

He looked at me. "Is there anything else you can tell me? Anything that seemed out of the ordinary?"

I shook my head. "Not that I can think of. Other than Tessa's death, things have been pretty ordinary."

He nodded. "Too bad a death had to ruin the festival. I was told numbers have been lower because of Tessa's death."

"Why?" Alec asked. "Has it been released to the press that she was murdered? A death caused by illness or accident shouldn't slow down the numbers."

What Alec said made sense. I was liking this Calvin guy less and less. It felt like he had decided to solve a murder whether or not there had been one.

Cal shrugged. "I guess it's hard to say. Maybe it's the economy. I'm only passing on the information I was given. Well, I don't want to take up any more of your time. I'll be in touch."

We watched him walk away. When he was out of earshot, I turned to Alec.

"You said he was a friend of yours? Because he doesn't seem like a friend," I said, narrowing my eyes at him.

"Well, I guess I'm using the term loosely." He shrugged and came around the back of the booth. "I guess I need to pick my friends more carefully."

"Do you really think Tessa was murdered? Does it seem to you like that's what happened?" I asked. If anyone would know, it would be Alec. He had spent over thirty years on the police force before retiring.

"I don't know. We really need that toxicology report. Until we get it, it's all just a guessing game."

"I just don't understand why Calvin is so determined to point to my cupcakes as being a possible murder weapon before he knows any of the facts about how Tessa died."

"He's being a detective. We're taught to over-think every shred of information, but we can be wrong. We're human," he said with a wink.

I nodded. At this point, I hoped Tessa hadn't been murdered. It would be easier for the family to deal with and it would be easier for Lucy and me. Cupcakes should never be accused of being murder weapons. They were too cute and tasty to be anything but fun.

Chapter Ten

"I DON'T UNDERSTAND this," I said, staring down at the muffins and strawberry cream cakes I had spent all last evening baking. "Why isn't anyone buying my desserts?"

"Maybe everyone's just out enjoying the festival," Lucy offered. "Don't worry about the desserts. They're very tasty."

It was late afternoon, and I had sold so little it made me sick. I would have to throw away a lot of food, not to mention how much work I had to put into making them.

"But everyone's out buying stuff. Lots of stuff. I see them walking by with their bags of goodies. Why aren't they buying my goodies?" I whined.

"I don't know, Allie. Those muffins are fantastic. So moist and fruity," Lucy assured me.

I sighed and tried to will the passing people to stop in and try my wares. Maybe if I concentrated really hard, it would work.

"Excuse me," I said to a passing threesome of young girls. "I've got samples. Would you like to try some muffins? They're the best at the festival."

They looked at me and giggled, moving on. I sighed again. What was going on here?

I jumped to my feet. "Free samples!" I called to a passing elderly couple. The man stopped and smiled at me.

"What kind of samples?" he asked.

"Strawberry apple muffins," I answered, picking up the glass lid so he could see them better.

The woman scowled at me. "Come on, George," she said, pulling on his arm.

I put the glass lid down again.

"I don't get it," I said. I turned to Alec and looked at him questioningly. "What is going on here?"

He shrugged. "I don't have a clue."

"Well, I'll tell you I will not sit here and feel sorry for myself. I will take a walk and feel sorry for myself. Want to come?"

"No, I will sit here and read my book," he said, holding his tablet up for me to see.

"Fine. Lucy?"

She shook her head. "You go ahead. I'll stay here."

"Okay. I'll bring you back something," I said, heading around to the back of the booth. "See if you can sell something while I'm gone."

"We'll give it our all," Alec said without looking up.

I sighed and walked along the rows of booths. Normally, I loved festivals. The booths were fun to check out and there were always lots of fun things to buy. I wished I knew why no one wanted to buy my fun things. Was I losing my touch? I doubted it, but maybe my age was catching up with me. I gasped. Was I becoming baking senile? Forgetting the things I had known since I was a girl? Maybe I had used salt instead of sugar in the muffins and no one wanted to tell me? No. That was ridiculous. I shook my head. I needed to stop thinking like this.

I approached Barnabas's booth and stopped.

"Hi Barnabas," I said and looked past him to the bottles near the back of the booth. "What kind of supplements do you sell?" I wondered if I needed some vitamins to give me more energy. Or maybe there was something I could take to improve my memory.

"I have a variety of all natural supplements. I'm constantly researching plants and supplements and I know a lot about what each plant does. Oh, say, have you tried American Ginseng? You said you ran the marathon, right?" he asked and went to the back of the booth. He picked up a bottle and brought it to me.

"Yes." I nodded and looked at the bottle he handed me.

"This helps long distance runners with stamina, endurance, and recovery."

"Do you grow and bottle all these supplements yourself?" I asked.

"Most of them. Some things I buy, but most I grow. Would you like a smoothie?"

I looked at the blender he pointed to. "Oh, no thank you."

"It's on the house. I've also been experimenting with maca powder and ginger. And of course, in the spirit of the festival, strawberries." Before I could say anything more, he dropped a handful of strawberries into the blender, followed by a heaping spoonful of the maca, American ginseng, and some ginger.

"It's been a few days since the marathon," I protested. "I'm recovering really well." It was true. Or at least I thought I was recovering well. Since I had never run a marathon before, I could only imagine that the leaden feeling in my legs was normal. It was nice of him to offer the smoothie, but I had eaten too many samples. I couldn't resist them when I saw them, and nearly every booth had some.

"But this will give you an energy boost. And it tastes delicious," he said, drizzling honey into it and pouring in coconut milk. "You will love this."

He switched the blender on and I smiled at him. The guy was a little pushy, and he loved his supplements.

"There we go," he said, switching off the blender. He picked up a plastic cup and poured the smoothie into it. "Try it."

"Okay, sure," I said. I didn't want to offend him, but I really didn't want to drink this stuff. I had heard of some of the supplements before, but I had never tried them and I had a feeling they might taste like weeds. I reluctantly took a sip and was pleasantly surprised when my taste buds lit up. "Wow, this is good." I took a bigger swallow.

"I told you," he said with a grin. "I know my smoothies. I also know that in order for people to try new, healthy things, it's got to taste good. Mission accomplished?"

I nodded and took another sip. "Mission accomplished. So what's it supposed to do again?"

"It drives oxygen to the muscles and helps in recovery. Of course, it would have been more helpful if you had drunk it right after the marathon, but I had run out of ingredients by the time you stopped by." He shrugged.

"I love it," I said. And I did. It had a wonderful fruity taste from the strawberries with a slight nutty background flavor. I could drink one of these every day. "I better buy some of that maca and American ginseng."

He nodded. "See? Give out free samples, and they buy."

"I guess it works for some people, but I have to say my samples are not getting people to buy. If someone would actually try my samples, they might buy my desserts, but no such luck."

"Oh?" he said, one eyebrow arched.

I nodded. I was embarrassed now that I had said it out loud. "I guess people are tired of strawberries."

"Nonsense. It's because people think you may have poisoned the young woman that died the other day. Everyone knows she ate one of your cupcakes."

I gasped. "What? What are you talking about?"

He nodded. "Sorry. I thought you knew. That little pixy looking woman seems to be telling people you poisoned the girl. They're all flocking to her booth to get the details. It turns out people will buy from you if you have a juicy story to tell."

I gasped louder. "Suzanna? That little French tart?"

He nodded. "I do believe she has an accent."

"Why that little—!" I said and stopped before I said something I would be sorry for. It figured. I should have seen it sooner. There were plenty of people flocking to her booth, but I didn't want to think about it when my own booth was miserably empty. "I will have a little talk with her."

"I don't believe you poisoned her. The young woman that died probably took illicit drugs or something. Young people are always taking drugs and doing things to endanger their health. Her death is her own fault."

I looked at him. What was he talking about? "She seemed healthy."

"Say, if you're interested, you should stop by my botanical gardens while you're in town for the festival. I have vitamins and herbs in my shop, and then there's the garden itself. It's very interesting if I do say so myself."

I stared at him. He switched topics quickly. "Yeah, sure," I said.

He handed me a flyer. "Here. It's easy to get to. I also have fresh honey from my own beehives. All organic, of course."

I nodded. "Yeah, maybe Alec and I will stop by." I looked toward Suzanna's booth and saw a crowd gathered around. My mouth went dry. That little woman was getting on my nerves and I would not stand for it anymore.

"I sure hope you'll stop by. I find athletes can benefit from supplementation far more than they know, if they only knew," he said and chuckled at his own joke. "Seriously. I think if an athlete is properly supplemented, they can improve their PR by leaps and bounds."

I turned back to him. "Yeah, okay," I said absently. I hardly heard a word he said. My mind was on more important things. "Thanks, Barnabas. I appreciate all your help. And I really appreciate the smoothie."

I turned and walked toward Suzanna's booth. She was going to get an earful.

The front of Suzanna's booth was crowded with people and I pulled up short. An image of me berating her in front of all those people sprang to mind, and I realized I might set myself up for a public lynching. They already thought there was a possibility I had killed an innocent young woman, and they might just snap if they saw me verbally attacking Suzanna. I turned around and went back to my booth to stew and decide what I should do.

Chapter Eleven

"LISTEN, YOU LITTLE French tart," I began, poking my finger at Suzanna. It was day five of the festival and I was about to have a showdown with Suzanna. She would think twice about spreading rumors about my food. "I know you're spreading rumors about my baked goods. And if you think I will sit quietly by and allow that to happen, you can forget about it."

Suzanna crossed her arms over her chest and smirked. "Why are you here?"

I could match her arrogant stance with my own arrogant stance. I put my hands on my hips, jutting one out to the side. "You know why. You're telling people the dead girl ate one of my cupcakes."

"And what's wrong with that?" she asked. "It's the truth."

"You don't know that. Just because she had pink frosting on her lips and a half-eaten cupcake in her booth, does not mean she ate one of my cupcakes. It's a strawberry festival and I'm sure other vendors have baked goods with pink frosting. You're spreading rumors so people won't buy any of my desserts."

"You don't know that for sure. Everyone's talking about the dead girl. Everyone. I'm simply telling what I know. She ate one of your cupcakes and then she died." She shrugged. "What else is there to tell?"

I gasped. "What you need to tell people is that you have no idea how she died, which is the complete and whole truth. What is wrong with you? I cannot believe you!" I wanted to stomp my feet and throw a tantrum, but I held it together.

"I'm sorry you do not approve of me telling what I know about the situation. But I dislike you, so I cannot lie for you."

I groaned inwardly. I could not stand this woman with her carefully coifed hair and her bright red lipstick. Not to mention her cute little French figure. It really was true that French women don't get fat. I had to run to keep from gaining weight from all those desserts I had to taste test, but I was sure she never exercised.

"You're telling people my baked goods are poison. That's slander."

She shrugged. "Call it what you want. I'm telling what I know about the situation."

"Suzanna. You're being ridiculous. Look, let's call a truce, shall we?" I suggested. "I won't tell everyone your desserts taste like cigarettes and you don't tell everyone the dead girl ate my cupcakes before dying."

She narrowed her eyes at me. "You tell people my desserts taste like cigarettes?"

I shrugged. "Maybe once or twice. Everyone knows Europeans like to smoke. It's a nasty habit."

She put her hands on her hips, cursed in French, and narrowed her eyes at me. "You fool. I have never smoked and my desserts taste pure and sweet and delicious. You're just jealous."

"Fine. Do we have a truce?"

She stared at me a moment. "Okay. We have a truce."

Nodding, I turned and left. I was not shaking hands on our agreement. It was doubtful she would keep her part of the bargain, anyway. Not that it would help with the festival almost over already, but Sandy Harbor wasn't that far away and her lie might spread. It would be the end of my baking career if it did.

"Well, what are you up to?" Alec asked when I got back to the booth.

"I'm bored. Let's go visit Barnabas's botanical garden thingy," I suggested. "Lucy, do you mind watching the booth?"

I needed to get away from this place. Suzanna had gotten on my last nerve and I needed a breath of fresh air.

"I don't mind," she said around a mouthful of strawberry scone.

"Come on," I said to Alec and headed to his car without looking over my shoulder to see if he was following.

THE GARDEN WAS ON THE outskirts of town and there was a big green and cream-colored sign out front. I had dropped by Barnabas's booth earlier that morning and the young woman running it said Barnabas had stayed at the shop to attend to business.

Alec held open the door to the shop for me and I entered. My eyes scanned the shop, and I smiled. The shop was quaint with shelves full of jars of supplements, jams, jellies, and honey. There was something cute and homey about it. Barnabas popped out from an aisle and gave us a big smile when he saw us.

"How wonderful!" he said. "I'm so glad you stopped by. Make yourselves at home. There are lots of things to see."

"Thanks," I said. "I told Alec how tasty the smoothie was that you made for me. I can almost swear my muscles feel better today."

"See? What did I tell you?" he gushed. "Maca is the biggest botanical secret on earth. It almost feels like a miracle. I'm a jogger, myself. I would never say I was a runner like the two of you, but I can jog with the best of them."

I smiled at him. Barnabas had a lot of energy and I wondered if it was due to his supplements and smoothies. I could use some of that energy.

"How long have you been in business?" Alec asked, looking over the products on the shelves. He stopped and picked up a jar and read the label.

"Almost fifteen years. I studied botany in college and came straight back here and got to work on my garden. A few years later I opened the shop. I needed to support the garden, you know."

I had to admit the place had a certain charm to it. The labels on the jars had a vintage look to them and added to the quaint feel of the place.

"So do you harvest and process the herbs here?" I asked.

He nodded. "Come see," he said and led the way to the back of the shop. He opened a door to a room, and I followed him. There were microwaves and a dehydrator inside and a supply of jars. Along one wall was a stainless steel sink, and a built-in dishwasher.

"Wow, you have quite the setup," I said, looking around.

"We have regular health inspections, of course," he said. "I have a license for handling foodstuffs. I wouldn't want to break any laws."

I nodded. "How interesting. So do you do a good business here?"

"I do very well. Sanford might not look it, but folks around here are very health-conscious. I suppose the marathon helps people to be more aware of physical fitness. Not to mention there are other races held throughout the year."

"That's great. I wish we had a place like this closer to Sandy Harbor," I said. "I have to buy most of my vitamins and supplements online."

Barnabas muttered 'tsk tsk' and shook his head. "All those supplements you buy online are old and stale. They lose most of their potency before they get to you."

"Do you think so?" I asked. I hadn't thought about it, but it made sense. They were probably stored in a warehouse for a while before being shipped out.

He nodded. "Come see," he said and led me out of the room. We headed into the shop and back to a display of dried fruits and vegetables. "I have plenty of foodstuffs. Healthy snacks. Fresh and dried herbs. When you buy from me, you get only the freshest."

I smiled. "That's great, Barnabas. I could see something like this working in Sandy Harbor. We have a lot of health-conscious people there."

"Perhaps I should branch out? Open a second store in Sandy Harbor?"

"That's not a bad idea. The drive wouldn't be too far for you to keep it supplied with herbs and supplements. You could hire someone local to run the shop. After they eat my desserts, they could stop by for something healthy."

He stopped smiling. "Desserts are fine for very rare occasions, but they shouldn't be indulged in too often. I'm surprised someone like you would indulge in a hobby like baking."

I stared back at him, unsure of what to say. "Well, ah, you know, it's in the blood. My grandmama taught me all I know about baking."

He waved a hand at me. "I suppose it can't be helped. Is that a Southern accent I hear?"

I nodded. "Alabama."

He sighed. "Those Southern people. They do like to eat."

My mouth dropped open. I closed it, and then opened it again to say something, but he turned and headed over to Alec.

"Have you found something you like?" he asked Alec.

"I did. I think I want to try some of the green tea extract," Alec said holding up a bottle to him.

I breathed out in exasperation as I watched Barnabas hurry over to Alec. Baking wasn't a hobby of mine. It was my life. It was my family's life. Giving it up would be detrimental to my well-being. What a depressing thought.

Chapter Twelve

IF SUZANNA HAD STOPPED telling people Tessa Brady was poisoned by my cupcakes, I couldn't tell it by the number of scones I sold. I had only sold two dozen by closing time. I sighed looking at all we would have to load back up into Alec's SUV and take home. Was it worth baking something for tomorrow's festival? There were two more days of the festival left and part of me hated to quit, but a bigger part of me hated to waste the time, energy, and money baking something that would go to waste. It hurt my little Southern heart that no one wanted my baked goods.

"Don't look so sad," Alec said, putting his arm around my shoulders. "It's just a fluke, and while it feels bad right now, it's temporary. These people will move on with their lives and forget who you are."

"Is that supposed to be comforting?" I asked.

"It's better than having your killer cupcakes seared into their minds, never to buy another baked good from you again."

I elbowed him in the ribs. He was right even though I hated to admit it. I hated the wasted time and energy, but at least this hadn't happened at home in Sandy Harbor.

"Okay. You're right. I need to move on."

He nodded. "That's my girl."

"Allie, what are you bringing tomorrow?" Lucy asked. "I told Ed he needed to come for the rest of the festival. Otherwise, I would buy everything I could get my hands on."

"I bet he'll be here then," I said. "I was debating on whether I would make something or not."

"Do it. Someone will buy your desserts. I feel like it's about to be your lucky day," Lucy said.

I chuckled. "Well, I'm sold then. I'll come up with something."

"That's the spirit," Alec said.

"Hey, isn't that Tessa's boyfriend Rich McGinty and her ex-best friend Tracie Jefferson?" I asked, watching them deep in conversation at Tracie's booth.

Alec turned to look. "Looks like it. I wonder what they're up to."

"I'm going to find out," I said and jumped to my feet. There must have been something in that smoothie Barnabas gave me because my muscles were feeling unusually fine. I wasn't completely over running 26.2 miles, but I felt a lot better. I grabbed a box of six scones and trotted over to Tracie's booth.

"Hey Tracie," I said. "How's business been?"

Tracie looked up at me, and if I wasn't mistaken, she looked guilty. "Oh, ah, not bad. Actually, I've sold a lot of soap and candles. I'm all out of the strawberry soaps."

"Wow, that's great. Wish I could say the same for my baked goods. I brought you over some scones. No use in them going to waste," I said holding the box out to her.

"Gosh, thanks. They look good," she said, peering in the little plastic window in the top of the bakery box.

I looked at Rich. "And how are the strawberry jam sales?"

He shrugged. "Not bad. I haven't been there much since, well, you know." He glanced at Tracie, and then looked away.

"Yeah, I still can't believe it happened," I said, nodding. "Have you heard anything new from the police? Do they know how she died?"

"No, they don't know anything. They think she might have had a heart attack, but she was awfully young for that."

"That surprises me they would even think about a heart attack," I said, furrowing my eyebrows. "She was so young. Your cousin said she didn't think she had any health issues."

"I'm not aware that she had any health issues," he said and glanced at Tracie again. "I mean, maybe she had an undiagnosed illness or something. That happens all the time."

"That's true," I said. "And with it being so sudden in someone that healthy, it's a really good probability."

"We need to get packing up," Tracie said. "I mean, I. I need to get packing up." Her eyes went to Rich, and then she turned away.

Something wasn't kosher here.

"So, Rich, how is Tessa's family doing? I know this has got to be hard on them."

His face went pale. "Yeah. I haven't really talked to them."

"What?" I asked. "What do you mean?"

"Well," he said, looking off into the distance. "I've never met Tessa's family. Her dad's the mayor, after all. He's busy." I watched as he fidgeted, putting his hands in his pockets and then pulling them out.

"Oh, I see. How long did you say you two were dating?" I asked. Tracie was packing up her soaps, and she slammed a box onto the table but didn't look up.

Rich jumped at the sound.

"Nine months," he said to me. "Well, we did date for a couple of months in high school. But you know, her dad was busy. We just never got to meet."

I was stunned. How did you date someone for nine months without meeting their family? Especially when they lived in the same town?

"I see," I said, and looked at Tracie. Her mouth was drawn into a tight line and she avoided looking at me. "Did she meet your family?"

"Yeah, she came to my parents' house for dinner a few times. Well, we've got to get packing up," he said and turned his back to me to pack up lip balm.

"Okay, well, enjoy those scones. If you need any help packing up, let me know," I said and took a few steps back. I waited for a response. When I got none, I turned and headed back to my booth.

"Well?" Alec asked when I sat on the chair beside him.

I put my finger to my lips and watched the two of them finish packing up.

I looked at Alec and then I nodded at the two of them. "What do you think?"

Alec crossed his arms across his chest and observed a few moments. "If I didn't know any better, I'd say she is one unhappy girl right now."

"That's what I think," I agreed. "I was asking about Tessa and she got angry. I realize they were no longer best friends before Tessa died, but for the sake of the former relationship, I would think she would feel bad about her death. She doesn't seem upset by it, though."

"What did he have to say?" Lucy asked.

"He said he and Tessa had been dating nine months but he never met her parents."

"Why wouldn't he have met her parents?" Lucy asked.

I shrugged. "She met his family, but he didn't meet hers. He said her father was too busy being the mayor to meet him."

"That's odd," Alec said. "Unless of course, he did meet her family and her family said he wasn't good enough. Maybe they didn't approve and told her to dump him."

"That's a possibility, but you know he looks like he might come from at least an upper middle-class family. He has moderately expensive looking clothes and that Audi he's driving isn't cheap."

Alec nodded. "True. Maybe Tessa didn't like him as much as he liked her and really didn't introduce him to her parents."

"And maybe Tessa wanted to break up with him and he took it hard. He may have killed her when he felt rejected," I suggested.

"Some people can't handle rejection," Lucy agreed.

We watched as Tracie and Rich put the rest of her soaps and lip balms into the trunk of her car. They stopped at the driver's side door and spoke for a minute. Tracie never smiled. She turned away, got into her car and drove off with Rich watching her go.

He turned and looked in our direction before heading to his own car.

"That's odd," I mused.

Alec nodded. "Let's get packed up. I'm tired and you have baking to do."

"You'll help, won't you?" I asked as he helped me to my feet.

"I might. Or I might just come over and watch you bake. I like that, you know."

"Yes, I do know that," I said, picking up a box of scones.

"You two are so cute with your baking talk," Lucy said.

"There's nothing like a nice romantic evening watching the one you love bake strawberry something or other," Alec said.

"As long as I get some help," I muttered, and carried three boxes of scones to Alec's SUV. I stowed them in the back and Alec came up behind me with four more boxes. It made me sad that I had so many left over. He leaned over and kissed my neck.

"Quit."

"Quit, what?" I asked him.

"Worrying over the unsold baked goods. It's a tiny setback. Everything will work out."

I nodded. "I know. Hey, let's stop by the homeless shelter on the way out and drop off these scones. It might be a nice treat for them."

"As long as they haven't heard you poisoned an innocent young girl with your cupcakes, I'm sure they'll appreciate it," he said with an evil gleam in his eye.

I narrowed my eyes at him. "Watch it, buddy, or you'll find a little surprise in your next cupcake."

He laughed and got into the car and I went around to the passenger side. I loved a man with a sense of humor. I hoped the rest of the festival was uneventful, but somehow I doubted that would happen.

Chapter Thirteen

DAY SIX BROUGHT STRAWBERRY pineapple upside down cake. Actually, they were cupcakes. I thought I had a better chance of selling small versions of pastries so people could walk around the festival and eat them. I had put a thin layer of pineapple on the bottom of each cupcake and a cherry in the center so when the cupcakes were inverted, the cherry and pineapple would be on top. I know. Genius. The strawberries were chopped and mixed into the batter. Each cupcake was a delightful little sweet package of fruity goodness.

"So, who's up for coffee?" I asked my sleepy headed crew.

"Me!" Lucy said, getting to her feet. "Let's go get some."

"You boys will be okay handling the customers? If we get customers?" I asked Alec and Ed.

Alec nodded. "Sure. We can handle it." He glanced over at Ed, whose chin was on his chest. He snored softly. The early mornings and the long drive were getting to us and caffeine was just what we needed.

"What can I get you?" I asked, picking up my purse and holding my hand out for the keys.

"Double shot of espresso with a little mocha mixed in for fun," Alec said, handing me the keys.

"Got it," I said and looked at Ed, who hadn't moved. "We'll get Ed a triple shot."

"That should do it," Lucy agreed.

We headed for Alec's SUV. I hoped Suzanna stuck to her word and stopped telling people I had poisoned Tessa. I was worried I would lose most of the money I had put into the festival. I wanted to quit, but Alec talked me into seeing it through, if for nothing more than being able to say I did it. I wasn't sure that was good reasoning, but I was going along with it.

WE STOOD IN LINE AT the local coffee shop and waited our turn. There was a long line of early birds waiting along with us.

"One thing I love about Maine is that every town is a small town," I said to Lucy as we waited. I watched as the people in front of me visited with one another.

"Ayuh, that's the truth," Lucy said laying the accent on thick and giving me a grin.

"I'm serious," I said. "I love that. Everyone's so friendly. If it hadn't been that way, I wouldn't have stuck around as long as I have." My husband had been Maine born and raised. We settled into his hometown of Sandy Harbor after college and marriage. I didn't think I would like it, being from Goose Bay, Alabama, but I had settled right in. Thaddeus had been the love of my life and losing him had nearly killed me. I thought I could never love again, but Alec had proved me wrong.

The door opened and closed behind me. I turned around to see Tracie get in line and I nudged Lucy. She glanced over her shoulder and then turned back raising her eyebrows at me.

"Hey, Tracie," I said as she waited behind us.

"Oh, hey," she said without a smile.

"How are you doing?" I asked her.

She shrugged. Today her hair was in braids and she looked even younger than she had before. I couldn't imagine her committing murder, but I had a hunch she might have. That was if Rich hadn't done it. I wished the toxicology would come back from the lab. Depending on what it was that killed Tessa, it might give us an idea of who had done it.

"I'm fine," she said, and her eyes went to the menu board at the front of the line.

We stepped forward as the line moved ahead.

"Ready for another day of great sales?" I asked, trying to get her to talk.

"Oh, sure. Festivals like this are great for homemade items. I guess you know that though."

I smiled and nodded. "Oh, sure," I said. I wished I knew it. If that pesky Frenchwoman kept her mouth shut, I might be able to salvage the week.

"Have you heard anything new about Tessa's death?" she asked.

That surprised me. I thought I would have to pry information out of her. "Not a whole lot. I don't think they have results from the autopsy yet. Poor thing. She was way too young to die."

She shrugged and rolled her eyes. "You have to go some time. Tessa was the kind of girl that never got what she deserved. But maybe this time, she did."

My eyes went wide. "You don't mean that," I said, lowering my voice.

"Yeah, I do. I told you that little tramp stole my boyfriend. Tessa was your typical cute rich girl. She took what she wanted without regard to anyone else's feelings."

"Really?" I asked, wide-eyed. I hoped I wasn't laying it on too thick, but she seemed willing to talk so I was going to encourage her if I could.

She nodded. "I don't know who killed her, but I'm sure it was because she did something to someone that just wasn't going to take it anymore."

"How do you know she was murdered?" I asked. No one knew for sure whether she was murdered or she died of health complications. Unless Tracie knew Tessa had been killed because she was the killer.

Lucy peered over my shoulder, waiting for the answer and we took four more steps forward as the line moved.

"I guess I don't," Tracie said, moving forward with us. "But knowing her, it wouldn't surprise me if she pushed someone too far."

"That's tough. Having to deal with someone like that," I said. I hoped sympathizing with her would get more out of her.

"You do not understand," she said. "I put up with her throughout high school and college. Seriously, when I heard she was going to the University of Maine, I almost transferred out of state. It wasn't worth dealing with her, but my parents couldn't afford out of state tuition. So I stayed. And I suffered for it."

"It seems a shame that a boy came between the two of you," I said. "You said you were friends once."

She shrugged. "We were friends when we were little. At the time I would have said best friends. But the truth was, we were only friends as long as I told her how wonderful she was. She could be mean even back then, and I was a sucker for letting her use me all those years."

"Do you and Rich get along now?" Lucy asked. "Being ex's and all, I could see where it could be awkward."

"Sure, I guess. He lives next door to my parents so I see him all the time."

I studied her somber face. She fell in love with the boy next door and her best friend stole him from her. In my opinion that made her a prime suspect.

"Well, maybe Rich is still interested in you," Lucy suggested.

I blinked. Did she just say that?

"I don't want him back," Tracie said, her jaw tightening. "He's tainted as far as I'm concerned. He came over to my booth last night and whined about losing Tessa. Do I look like I care?"

"Nope, you sure don't," I conceded.

"Nope. I sure don't," she agreed.

"Well, her death is a stain on the name of the festival," I said. "I suppose city officials are worried about that since it draws so many people and brings in a lot of money."

She shrugged. "I don't care. As long as I make back the booth fee and some spending cash, I'm good with it."

"Do you sell soaps full time?" I asked her.

"Part-time. I work at the Pizza Shoppe over on Broadmoor and make soaps at night to sell online. I occasionally do fairs and festivals to make extra money," she said.

"You got a college education and you work at a pizza place?" I asked. Something didn't add up.

"What's wrong with that? I'm the manager. I make okay money."

"Oh, well that makes sense then," I said. Sort of. Fast food didn't seem to be the sort of job a college-educated woman would look for. How did you explain to your parents that you got a job in fast food after they paid for your education?

The line moved faster, and we got to the counter and placed our order. We said goodbye to Tracie on the way out and got into Alec's SUV.

I turned and looked at Lucy. "What do you think?"

"I think Tracie has as good a reason to murder Tessa as anyone. I have to wonder if she wants Rich back."

"That's what I think. The more I find out about Tracie, the more I wonder if she and Rich were in cahoots together," I said.

She nodded. "I bet that's what happened. Once they got rid of Tessa, they were free to date again."

"But why didn't he just break up with Tessa? Why kill her?" I wondered.

"Tracie makes her out to be a spoiled rich girl. Maybe he tried to break up with her and she refused to go."

"Maybe she got her daddy, the mayor, involved and things got ugly. A spurned rich girl can be trouble," I said.

I sighed. We needed that toxicology report. It might answer at least some of the questions we had about Tessa's murder.

Chapter Fourteen

"THAD! SARAH!" I SCREECHED when we got out of the car. "I'm so glad you came!" I ran to the booth, trying not to spill the cups of coffee in my hands.

Thad was my son and Sarah was his fiancée. They had both been away at college in Wisconsin. I knew they were due to arrive home for the summer after visiting Sarah's parents, but I was surprised to see them here so early.

"Hey, Mom," Thad said as I pulled him to me in a tight hug. He gasped. "Mom, I need air."

"You're such a comedian," I said, pushing him aside and hugging Sarah. "I'm glad to see you, Sarah."

"Me too, Allie. We were going to wait for you to come home and surprise you tonight, but we decided to take a drive out here instead."

"That's wonderful. Oh, I wish I'd have known. I would have brought you coffee. Do you want me to go back and get you some?"

"No, we had some on the way up, thanks though," Sarah answered. "How's the festival been?"

"Not bad. Lots and lots of strawberries," I said, and handed Alec his coffee.

Lucy gave Thad and Sarah a hug and nudged Ed awake, handing him his coffee. "Hope you guys love strawberries. They're so sweet this year."

"Love them. Have you sold much?" Thad asked, looking at me.

I frowned. "No. It seems a certain Frenchwoman from a certain French restaurant in Sandy Harbor has a booth here at the festival. She told everyone the young woman that died here the other day ate one of my cupcakes right before she keeled over. FYI, there was a woman that died here the other day."

"Dang. That's just mean," Thad said with a wicked grin on his face.

"It's more than mean, it's twisted. Has business picked up any since I've been gone?" I asked Alec, hopefully.

"We've sold three upside down cupcakes," Alec said, "We've had a lot of people stop for samples, though. That's looking up from the past few days, so maybe customers will stop by before the festival is over."

"That sounds promising," I said. "Let's hope they do."

"Hey Mom, how is it that dead bodies keep turning up everywhere you go?" Thad asked. "People drop like flies around you."

"They don't, smarty pants," I said leaning against the booth. "It just seems that way."

"What did she die of?" he asked.

"They haven't gotten the toxicology report back yet. It's possible there was a caustic substance involved. Or it could be she was allergic to something," Alec answered.

"Huh. I thought it was my mom's baking."

"Thanks for the vote of confidence, Thad," I said. "For that, you aren't getting any strawberry upside down cake."

"Too late, I helped myself while you were gone."

I rolled my eyes at him. The kid was a smart aleck, but I don't know where he got it from. I swear, I don't.

"Alec, we ran into Tracie at the coffee shop," I told him.

"And?" he asked.

"It seems she really did not like Tessa Brady and hasn't lost a wink of sleep over her death."

"Yeah, Tracie said Tessa had tormented her ever since she stole her boyfriend," Lucy added. She lifted the lid on the sample plate and snitched a square of the strawberry upside down cake. "Mm, this is good."

"If you ask me, I think she's guilty of something," I said.

"We don't know for sure if Tessa was murdered," Alec reminded me.

"But it seems kind of obvious with the foaming at the mouth and the caustic burns," I pointed out.

"That sounds terrible," Sarah said, wrinkling up her nose.

"Doesn't it though?" I asked. "Poor thing. She was a cute girl about your age and in great shape. I can't see how it could be anything other than murder."

"We need to wait and find out for sure," Alec said, taking a sip of his coffee. He grimaced. "That is strong coffee."

"You asked for a double shot," I reminded him. "It should be an eye opener."

"Did she say anything else?" Alec asked.

"Only that Rich was the boy next door, and she fell in love with him. Tessa stole him from her. She says she's over him and doesn't want him back, but I have my suspicions that may not be true."

I looked over in the direction of Tracie's booth. I could just see the top of her head from where I sat. "Come on, Sarah, Lucy, we need some strawberry soap."

We got to our feet and wandered down the line of booths, weaving in and out of people. We stopped at Tracie's booth and looked over the soaps and candles. Tracie was with a customer, so we waited.

"I like this one," Sarah, said holding a bar of strawberry honey soap to her nose. "It smells so fresh."

I nodded. "I bought some of her candles. Everything she sells is wonderful smelling."

Tracie finished up with her customer and wandered over to where we stood admiring her soaps.

"Seems like we keep running into each other," she said, giving me a smile.

"I know, right?" I said. For a woman that might have just murdered someone, she seemed calm. I never got over the fact that killers could be so cold-hearted. If I ever murdered someone, I was sure I would be shaking and crying so hard there would be no way to cover up what I'd done.

"I like this lemon one," Lucy said, picking up a yellow bar.

"That one has olive oil in it. It's good for your complexion," Tracie offered. "There's one with lemon, sage, and thyme, in it too. It's more of a savory scent than a sweet one. It's very nice."

"I see," Lucy said, picking up a yellow bar with green herbs in it.

"I see you have more of the strawberry soaps in," I pointed out.

"Yeah, I stayed up late last night and made some. It doesn't take long. I cut the bars first thing this morning."

I was wondering if I hadn't gone into the wrong business. Soap making looked like it could be fun without the hazard of excess calories. I could come up with all different kinds of recipes, just like I did with desserts. If Suzanna ran my business into the ground with her lies, soap making might be a good alternative.

"I love all of these soaps," Sarah said, picking up a purple bar and smelling it.

"Blackberry and thyme," Tracie supplied.

"I'll add it to my stack," Sarah said, putting it down with four other soaps she had chosen.

"You ladies are good for my business," Tracie said and laughed. "Let me give you a business card. It has my web address on it." She reached under the booth table and searched around in her purse. I glimpsed a dark colored bottle in her purse. She zipped it up tight, and I looked at her. What was that? It wasn't anything I recognized, but it looked odd, like an old apothecary bottle from years ago. "Here you go." She handed each of us a card with her web address on it.

"That's great," I said. "I love what you do here. You're very creative with the scent combinations."

She beamed. "Thank you. I appreciate that. Last year I worked for that guy in the booth down the way and learned a lot."

"Barnabas?" I asked.

She nodded. "He's kind of creepy, but he's very good with herbs and botanicals. I learned a lot from him, but then I realized I was better at creating different kinds of soaps, so I quit to start my own business."

"Why do you say he was creepy?" I asked.

She shrugged. "I don't know. Just a vibe. Tessa worked there, too. He seemed to have a thing for her, but then, a lot of guys did." She looked away and arranged some of the soaps on the booth table.

"That must have been difficult if you didn't get along with Tessa," I said.

She sighed and looked at me. "It was awful. But I learned a lot about herbs and because I worked there, I was able to start my own business. So in the end, I guess it was worth it."

"Did Tessa like Barnabas's attention?" I asked, picking up a pale green bar of soap and smelling it.

"Honey lime," she said of the soap. "She couldn't stand him. But it's not like we had girl-to-girl chats about it. I could just tell. Tessa was fake-nice to him to keep the job though. She was fake-nice about a lot of things."

I nodded. "Barnabas seems to know a lot about botanicals," I said. "And you're very creative with the soaps." I wondered about her saying Barnabas was creepy. Sometimes I got the same vibe, and other times I thought he was fascinating with all he knew about herbs and plants. And then there was his interest in Tessa. Had he been too interested?

"You should try to sell your soaps in local shops. Maybe you could offer a shop owner a commission on each bar sold in exchange for selling your items," Lucy suggested to Tracie. She had three bars in her hand and was eyeing a fourth. These soaps were addicting.

I glanced over at Rich's booth. He was sitting at the table, looking forlorn. I didn't know whether to feel sorry for him or think of him as a killer.

Chapter Fifteen

"GUESS WHAT?" ALEC ASKED me.

I turned to him as I packed up the rest of the strawberry upside down cakes. "What?"

"Barnabas asked us to dinner at the seafood place down on the highway. I said yes." There was a smile on his face as he told me.

I gasped. "Now? Tonight?"

He nodded. "Yeah. I figured it would give us a chance to unwind before driving home, and we need to eat, anyway. Plus, he said he'd pay, so why not?"

"You have got to be kidding me. You're not serious, right?" I asked as I dumped the rest of the samples into the trashcan behind the booth. Business had been a little better today. Even better was the fact that I hadn't seen Suzanna all day. Thad, Sarah, Lucy, and Ed had all left earlier, and we were finishing packing up.

"No, why would I kid you?" he asked innocently.

"Alec, we don't even know the man," I pointed out. "Why do I want to have dinner with him?"

He shrugged. "He had some interesting ideas on athletes and nutrition. I wanted to hear more of it. Don't you? Maybe he has something that will help us with our next marathon."

I tilted my head. "I hurt so bad from the last marathon that I don't think I will ever run another one."

"That's what everyone says right after a marathon, whether it's the first one or not. Three weeks later, they're checking their calendar to see when they can squeeze in another one. Trust me, you'll feel differently about it. And if Barnabas has something that will help with soreness, or even better, speed, I would like to know."

I sighed and looked up to the heavens. I was just plain tired. It had been a long week, and it wasn't over yet. I looked him in the eye. "Can you promise me you won't let the evening get dragged out? That we can go home at a reasonable time?"

He nodded. "We can. But you might want to text Jennifer and see if she can whip up something to sell tomorrow. Just in case."

I groaned. Poor Jennifer. She had been such a sport to handle all the baking that went to Henry's Home Cooking Restaurant, plus some of what I had brought to the festival. I hoped she wasn't all out of strawberry recipes. I pulled my phone out of my pocket.

I SAT ACROSS FROM BARNABAS and put a smile on my face. As tired as I was, he was still a pleasant person to talk to, so I tried to suck it up and be happy.

"Ashwagandha root," Barnabas said with finality.

"Excuse me?" I asked. He was looking at me like I should understand what he was talking about.

"Ashwagandha root is a little-known herb that helps with athletic endurance and recovery."

"Oh. What is it?" I asked.

"An herb that can be dried and ground into a powder and put into capsules. Or added to food. It's also used to help you relax."

My brows arched in interest. "So, we could put it in cookies and make it tasty and it would help athletic performance?"

He nodded.

"So cookies would then be health food, right?" I asked. I was reaching here, but I didn't care. I needed an excuse to keep up with my baking habit.

He frowned. "No. Cookies will never be healthy. But you could make a healthy cookie without sugar or added fat and put the powdered Ashwagandha root into it. Then, it would be a healthy cookie." He smiled and his eyes lit up at the idea.

I shook my head. "I like real cookies, not those pretend cookies with no sugar or fat."

"Allie is an excellent baker," Alec added. "Have you tasted any of the desserts she's brought to the festival?"

"Oh, no," Barnabas said, pursing his lips together. "I would never poison my body with sugar or trans fats."

My eyes went wide. "Seriously? Never?"

He shook his head. "My body is a temple."

I tried not to be obvious in looking him up and down, but I was pretty sure his string-bean frame was not a temple. A hut in the desert, maybe. But not a temple.

"I think you're missing out on some of the best parts of life," I said. "Food is something to be celebrated and enjoyed."

"Food can kill," he said, giving me a hard look. "So many modern diseases are caused by food. Just take a look around you at all the unhealthy people in the world."

"What about your jams and jellies?" I asked.

"I use all natural ingredients. Honey, or concentrated juices to sweeten them. No sugar."

I looked at Alec for help. This guy had a dreary life. Who doesn't love a good cupcake?

"Allie learned to bake from her grandmama in Alabama," Alec pointed out. "It's family tradition, and quite important to her."

Barnabas took a deep breath. "I'm sorry. I didn't mean to appear rude. I understand that food can be enjoyed and should be. I suppose I've spent my life working on discovering the key to health and sometimes I forget the rest of the world doesn't live like I do." He smiled. "My grandmother died at a young age. Fifty-seven. She had cancer and a good many food-related allergies, and I loved her so. It made me want to discover how to cure disease with food, or at least, with natural supplements."

I nodded. Now it made sense. Really, Barnabas was doing something similar to what I was doing. I celebrated and remembered my grandmother by doing what she loved. Baking. And he celebrated and remembered his grandmother by trying to find something that might have saved her.

"I can understand that," I said. "Completely."

He nodded. "Yes, I see the connection," he said and chuckled. "Look at us. We're just sentimental fools at heart, aren't we?"

"We are," I agreed.

"Have you tried out this Ashwagandha root?" Alec asked.

"I've used it and I have to say, it's promising. But one person does not a study make. I need more volunteers. But I am keeping copious notes on what I'm doing and searching the Internet for more case studies."

"That's fascinating," Alec said. "I'd love to see your data sometime."

"Of course!" Barnabas said. His eyes lit up, and he seemed almost giddy at the prospect. "We can go to my shop after dinner and take a look at it."

I groaned inwardly and looked at Alec.

"I'm sorry, it's getting late and we still have a drive ahead of us, but maybe in the next day or two?" Alec asked.

He nodded. "Oh, of course. I know you have to drive home. Feel free to drop by anytime though."

I smiled and cut off a piece of my deep fried fish with my fork, dipped it into some lovely fatty tartar sauce, and took a bite. Thankfully, Alec was a smart cookie and hadn't said yes to him. He would have been in hot water, otherwise. I looked at Barnabas' plate. Broiled salmon and steamed zucchini, no butter. He took the healthy eating thing a little far if you asked me. He was thin as a rail and a little fried fish might have done him some good. Plus, it was tasty.

"So, have you heard anything about the young woman that died at the festival?" Alec asked him.

I looked at Alec, but he kept his eyes on his plate of broiled scallops. Dipped in drawn butter, of course. My man knew how to live.

Barnabas dropped his fork on his plate with a clatter. I looked up at him as he squinted his eyes shut. I wasn't sure if he had a sudden headache or the subject of Tessa's death was painful.

Alec looked at him, questioning.

Barnabas smiled. "I can't imagine why that's of any importance. It was her time to go, right?" He picked up his fork and speared a piece of zucchini and put it in his mouth.

I glanced at Alec. For someone that was convinced he could help extend people's lives with botanicals, it was odd Barnabas suddenly thought it was Tessa's time to go when she had been so young and healthy.

Alec watched him, then took a sip of his water and glanced at me. I shrugged.

Chapter Sixteen

WE HAD FORGOTTEN PAPER plates and napkins and in the hopes I could move some strawberry cheesecake, I made a quick trip to the local grocery store. I was pushing my shopping cart down the paper goods aisle when I ran into Rich McGinty.

"Hi Rich," I said, walking up behind him. He was perusing the floral paper napkins, and he jumped like he'd been poked with a pin.

He turned and stared at me a minute before answering. "Oh, hey, Allie. How are you?"

"I'm well, thank you. I can't believe I forgot paper plates and napkins. So, here I am. What are you up to?"

"The same thing. I needed napkins," he said motioning toward the shelf.

I smiled. "Rich, how are you doing? I mean, how are you really doing? I know this has got to be so hard on you." I wanted to be sympathetic to him in case he was innocent. But if he wasn't, I thought asking him questions about Tessa might push him over the edge. Maybe his guilt would make him confess.

He shrugged and looked away. "I'm fine."

"You know, I used to write a blog on grief. My husband was killed by a drunk driver eight years ago. I don't add new articles to it anymore, but I left the blog and all of its content up. It might help you deal with the loss of Tessa."

He looked at me and his eyes looked a little moist. "It's been really hard."

"Here, let me get you a card," I said, digging in my purse. I kept a supply of business cards with the blog address on it for occasions like this. I pulled it out and handed it to him.

"Thanks. I'll have to check it out," he said, looking the card over. Then he looked at me. "I still can't believe she isn't going to text me any minute."

I nodded. "I understand the feeling completely. When someone leaves you, it feels surreal in the beginning. You keep waiting for them to walk around the corner or call you, or text you. I understand."

He gave me a tight-lipped smile. "It makes it kind of hard since I never met her parents. I feel like I don't matter to anyone in her family."

I looked at him, tilting my head. "Why is that, Rich? I know you said it was because her father is the mayor and he's busy, but it seems like he could have squeezed a few minutes in to meet his daughter's boyfriend."

He returned my gaze for a moment. "I don't know. I asked her about it all the time. I thought I was important to her."

"I'm sorry," I said. He seemed genuinely sad about the whole thing. Maybe I had been rash in thinking he had something to do with Tessa's death.

"Thank you," he said and looked away again.

"Did she seem like she wanted a future with you?"

"She said she did. We talked about where we might settle down. She wanted to move to California. No snow, she said." He gave me a grim smile. "I told her I'd go wherever she wanted me to go. As long as she was with me, it didn't matter."

He was breaking my heart. "Don't let yourself feel too badly about not meeting her family. There may have been a good reason for it. Maybe she didn't have a good relationship with them and she wanted to spare you that," I suggested. Things didn't add up, but he seemed sincere. I couldn't imagine a murderer being that good at acting. I could have been wrong, but Rich didn't seem like a murderer.

"Yeah. That's what I've been telling myself." He shrugged. "It's not like it matters now. She's gone."

"Are you and Tracie good friends?" I asked. I figured if I could get insight into his relationship with Tracie I might find some clues to what happened to Tessa.

"We dated a while. It wasn't anything serious. We lived next door to each other for years and I guess she had a crush on me. She was Tessa's best friend when they were younger. I guess Tracie took it pretty hard when we broke up and I started dating Tessa. I didn't mean to hurt her, but I just didn't have the same feelings she had for me."

"That's a tricky situation," I said.

He nodded. "But we've been talking and I think maybe she's forgiven me. I think Tessa's death hit her hard, and she's realizing she doesn't want to hold on to anger over the past. You never know when it's your time to go."

"Really?" I asked. It was out of my mouth before I knew what I was saying.

He nodded. "Yeah. I think she wishes she could have another chance to let Tessa know she doesn't hold anything against her. She really cared about Tessa and she's sorry she died."

"That's really good," I said, nodding. I was having a hard time understanding how he could believe that, unless Tracie was trying to get him to think she had nothing to do with Tessa's murder. Every time I had talked to her, her bitterness toward Tessa came through loud and clear.

"Well, I better get going. I've got a booth to run," he said. "My cousin is probably getting tired of doing all the work."

"I'll see you down at the festival," I said and watched him grab a package of floral paper napkins and head off.

I tossed some napkins and paper plates into my own cart, then pushed the cart down the aisle and picked up plastic cups, Coke, and ice and headed to the checkout.

"GUESS WHO I RAN INTO at the store?" I asked Alec. Lucy and Ed had taken the day off so we were on our own.

"Who?" he asked, helping me with the items I had bought at the grocery store.

"Rich. We talked a few minutes. It seems he thinks Tracie is over being mad at him for dumping her and dating Tessa. He also thinks Tracie has forgiven Tessa for dating him and she wishes she could tell Tessa that. I tried to keep my eyes from popping out of my skull when he said it, but I don't think I succeeded."

"Huh. I thought Tracie was still bitter about the whole thing."

I set the napkins beside the samples of cheesecake. "That was my impression. I'm pretty sure she's very bitter, in fact."

"So, Rich thinks she's fine with it, but Tracie clearly isn't. Why would he lie?"

"Or, why would Tracie lie to him and pretend she's fine with everything and that she forgives Tessa when she doesn't?" I asked, opening a folding chair and setting it upright.

Alec nodded. "Something doesn't add up."

"I will say Rich seems sincere when he talks about Tessa. He's pretty hurt about Tessa's family not wanting anything to do with him."

"I don't understand them not wanting to meet him. I still think the mayor looks down on him for some reason," Alec said, putting ice into a plastic cup and pouring Coke into it. "Soda?"

"Coke," I corrected him and sat down. "Have you heard from Calvin? Anything new?"

He shook his head. "Not a thing. I'm glad this festival is nearly over. I'd like to hang out around the house, put my feet up, and watch a baseball game."

"I know," I said. "You've been such a good sport, coming here with me every day. I appreciate that."

"Tomorrow's a special day, you know."

"It is?" I asked, trying to think of what that could be.

He nodded. "It's the last day of the festival."

"I see," I said, taking the cup from him. "I guess you could say you're really looking forward to the end of the festival?"

He nodded. "That, and so much more."

"What do you mean?" I asked.

He shrugged. "I don't know. I guess we'll have to wait and see."

I narrowed my eyes at him. "That sounds suspicious."

"I don't know what you're talking about. Oh, look. Here comes a customer. Offer him a sample."

A teenager wearing a baseball hat approached the booth, and I jumped to my feet. "Would you like a to try a sample of cheesecake?"

Chapter Seventeen

WE UNLOADED THE CAR for the last day of the festival. I was a little sad, as ridiculous as that sounded. I was taking a liking to the town and thought I might even miss it a little. It was the city of my first marathon after all, and Sanford would always hold a sweet place in my heart. I think.

"So, this is it," I said as I set out the sample plate with chunks of strawberry donuts. I had drizzled a thin strawberry glaze on them and they smelled delicious. It had been forever since I made donuts and it was a nice change of pace.

"This is it," Alec said with a grin.

"What are you grinning about?" I asked him and put my arms around him.

He looked into my eyes and giggled like a schoolgirl.

"What is that for?" I asked him. He was acting awfully giddy. Maybe he was as glad to be done with the festival as I was.

He shrugged. "I'm just happy to be near you. I think I'll sing you a song. How about 'Happy Together'?"

"I would love to hear you sing," I said, giggling along with him. His giddiness was contagious.

"That's too bad, because I can't sing."

He pulled away and sat on one of the folding chairs.

"That's a disappointment," I said and put six boxes of donuts on the table. Jennifer had finished making the donuts by the time I got home the night before and I was too tired to make a second baked good for the festival, even though things had picked up considerably. Suzanna must have been true to her word and stopped telling people my cupcakes had poisoned Tessa.

"There's Lucy and Ed," Alec said as they pulled up beside his SUV.

"Oh, good. They've been troopers. I need to get them a little thank you gift for all they've done this week."

"Ayuh," Alec said, and turned his tablet on.

"Reading anything good?" I asked him.

"A mystery," he said without looking up. "Seems there's a nosy female sleuth in the mix."

I snorted and turned away from him. "Hi, Lucy, Ed," I said as they entered the booth.

"Hi, Sweetie," Lucy said.

"Hey," Ed echoed.

"Donuts!" Lucy said, peering at the sample plate.

"Yup, and that's all. I'm tired. If they missed out on all the other strawberry treats I made, it's their loss." I guess you could say my attitude was suffering a little. And I still needed a nap.

"I'm not missing out," Ed said, taking a whole donut from a box. He sat down on one of the folding chairs and gazed at the donut lovingly before taking an enormous bite. His eyes closed in ecstasy as he slowly chewed the donut.

"I take it you approve of my donuts, Ed," I said.

He nodded without answering and took another bite.

"Why don't we go for one last walk?" Lucy asked me. "Ed still has some money left and I need to remedy the situation."

I giggled. "Let's go."

"It's such a pretty day," Lucy said as we walked along the booths.

"That's weird. Barnabas isn't here today," I said, looking at his empty booth.

"Maybe he had something else he had to do," Lucy said. "Don't you find him a little odd?"

"I guess a little. But he's really quite nice. We went to dinner with him and he's very intent on health and nutrition. He got into studying plants and health because his grandmother died of cancer. He's searching for a natural cure for cancer."

"I don't know about that. I just don't think cancer can be cured by something natural," Lucy said.

"Maybe not. But I guess he's on a mission of some sort."

We went to Tracie's booth and looked over what she had left.

"Hi," she said. "Last day. I'm kind of glad."

I nodded. "I'm thinking the same thing."

"What's that in those bottles?" Lucy asked, pointing to a display of six dark blue bottles. "I don't remember seeing those before."

"Oh! I was experimenting with different ingredients last night and came up with something new. It's a lotion with witch hazel, aloe vera, and lemon verbena. All three are good for the skin, and help clear up blemishes."

She handed Lucy a bottle, and I looked at it with her. Lucy removed the lid, and we smelled it.

"It has a nice scent," I said. "Do you just try different combinations of ingredients until you come up with something you like?"

She nodded. "I've been doing this a while so I know a lot about the ingredients. I had these bottles left over from something I made a while back and I printed up some labels. Now I've got a new product."

"I think I'll buy a bottle for my daughter. She still has occasional breakouts," I said.

I paid for the lotion and we moved on. There were still a lot of booths, but I noticed a few had shut down early. I wondered if Suzanna had spread rumors about them, too.

"I know she did it," a woman in front of us said.

"I know, I know. But what are you going to do? The police are working on finding enough evidence to arrest her," the man she was with said. They looked to be in their early sixties and they strolled along, not paying attention to us. I nudged Lucy, and we took a couple steps closer and followed them.

"We don't need more evidence," the woman said. "She's hated Tessa ever since Rich broke up with her. I don't know what the police are waiting for. They need to arrest her."

"It will happen. Have patience," the man said.

The woman sighed. "We had better steer clear of her. I don't know what I'll do if I come face to face with her."

I glanced at Lucy.

"Mr. Mayor, how's it going?" An older man leaning against a booth called to the man in front of us.

The mayor nodded in the other man's direction. "Just fine. Just fine. It's been a wonderful festival."

I turned and looked at Lucy and she stared back at me wide-eyed.

We hurried along behind them, trying to hear what they were saying, when a woman stopped them. "I'm so sorry for your loss," she said, frowning.

The mayor and his wife nodded and thanked her, but kept moving.

They stopped off at a booth selling fresh strawberries and went behind it to sit down. The man running the booth leaned over and whispered something to the mayor and he nodded.

"How about that," I whispered to Lucy. We went to the booth and looked over the strawberries, pretending that was what we were there for. I hoped they would say something more, but they were quiet. Smiling, but not saying much.

"I'm sorry," I said, addressing the man and his wife. "I'd like to extend my condolences on the loss of your daughter."

"I'm so sorry," Lucy said.

The mayor and his wife wore dark sunglasses and hats with large brims. They smiled politely and nodded. "Thank you," his wife said. "We appreciate that."

I nodded, and we left. I didn't know them and it felt awkward to try to engage them in further conversation. I would have liked to have continued eavesdropping, but I couldn't think of a reason to stand there any longer.

"I feel terrible for them," Lucy said as we walked back to the booth.

"Me, too. It sounds like they blame Tracie for Tessa's death. I hope she doesn't run into them today."

"Wouldn't that be terrible?" Lucy said.

"It could get ugly," I agreed. "I wonder where Rich is today."

"Yeah, we haven't seen him. This whole thing is just plain odd," she said. "Still no word on the autopsy?"

"Not a word," I said. "Alec needs to check in with his buddy Calvin before we leave today. I'd like to know if they've figured out anything new, and I can't wait to leave Cal behind for good."

"I'd like to leave it all behind," Lucy said.

"I can't argue with that," I agreed. "But I hope they find Tessa's killer. She deserves justice."

"I completely agree."

I kept going back and forth over the things we had discovered about Tessa's death. Was Tracie the killer? Or was it Rich? Or maybe someone we hadn't considered. Alec would point out that we didn't know if a murder had occurred, but I had my own ideas on that.

Chapter Eighteen

WE HURRIED BACK TO the booth to talk to Alec, but Ed was sitting in the booth by himself when we got there.

"Where's Alec?" I asked, disappointed.

"That detective friend of his came and talked to him. They wandered off somewhere."

"Speak of the devil," I said to Lucy. "Where did they wander off to? Alec didn't tell me he was going anywhere."

Ed shrugged. "I don't know. Alec said he'd be back shortly and told me to mind the store. That's what I'm doing."

He had a donut in one hand and was staring at the phone in his other hand.

"He'll be back, and maybe he'll have some new information about Tessa," Lucy said, patting my shoulder.

I sat down on a chair to pout. I had information to tell him and he was off investigating without me. Not that I wanted to spend time around Calvin. That guy got on my nerves.

"Oh, and that detective said he wanted to question you two again," Ed said without looking up.

"What?" Lucy asked, lifting the lid on the sample plate. "Question us about what? We told him all we know."

I rolled my eyes. "I have nothing new to tell him. He needs to do his job and find the killer instead of harassing us."

"You can say that again," Lucy agreed.

I pulled my phone out of my pocket and texted Alec, asking him where he was. After five minutes of willing him to text back, I gave up and put my phone back in my pocket.

I leaned against a pole in the corner of the booth and wished it was the end of the day. I was done with this festival.

My phone went off, and I jumped. I pulled it back out of my pocket.

I'm with Cal. You and I have an invitation to have lunch with Barnabas at noon at his place. I'll meet you there.

I grimaced and texted him back.

I don't really want to have lunch with Barnabas. Can't we just eat with Ed and Lucy?

I stared at the phone until he responded.

I already promised him. It's our last day here and it won't hurt. I wanted to see the studies he's found on herbs and athletic performance. I'll meet you there.

"What is it?" Lucy asked.

"Alec promised Barnabas we'd meet him for lunch."

"That's nice," she said and reached for a whole donut.

"I guess. I'm just ready for this day to be over. Sorry I'm such a whiner."

"It's okay. It's what I expect from you," she said holding the donut to her nose and inhaling.

I narrowed my eyes at her. Smarty pants.

I DROVE ALEC'S CAR over to Barnabas' shop. I really wasn't looking forward to spending time alone with Barnabas and I hoped Calvin had already dropped Alec off. I didn't want to entertain Barnabas on my own.

I pushed on the shop door, but it was locked. Then I noticed the closed sign in the window. That was odd. Barnabas hadn't been at the festival and I thought it might have been because he was running his shop. I turned to head back to the car when he popped out from the side of the shop.

"Hello, Allie," he said, out of breath.

I screamed. "Oh, Barnabas. You startled me."

"I'm sorry," he said putting his hands up. "I didn't mean to startle you. I heard your car, and I came to see who it was. Did Alec tell you I invited you for lunch?"

I nodded. "Yes, that's why I'm here. He told me to meet him here." I forced myself to smile. Alec had better not let me down. I'd go looking for him if he took too long to get here.

"Oh? Is he tied up somewhere?"

I nodded. "Yes, his friend stopped by and they went, well, to do something. I don't know exactly what. But he'll be here soon."

He nodded. "Of course. Some things can't be helped."

"So, Barnabas, I was surprised when you weren't at your booth today. I hope nothing's wrong."

"Oh, no. Nothing's wrong. I intended to be there, but then one thing led to another, and I got tied up here at the store. Then I decided I might as well cook lunch and invite my new friends over to enjoy it with me. No reason to waste the day."

"That was very kind of you," I said, and waved away a bee. "Is your shop normally closed on Saturdays?"

He shrugged. "Sometimes."

He didn't offer any other explanation, and I smiled at him in the awkward silence.

"Why don't we go for a walk in the garden while we wait? I have lunch cooking and we have some time to kill," he suddenly said. He motioned to the back of the shop and I followed after him.

Once we were beyond the shop, there was a packed dirt trail that led through a set of double gates. From the outside, the garden looked a little like a jungle with tall trees that had branches hanging down. The chain link fence surrounding it had tall spindly trees and vines growing along it and the plants seemed to grow wild.

"This is your garden?" I asked, trying to take it all in.

"Yes, please follow along behind me," he said. "I have so many varieties of plants here, I think you'll be impressed."

"It looks like it," I said, nodding.

When we walked through the gates, I saw there was more order to the garden than I first thought. Many plants were growing in rows and in planters off the ground. Markers stuck in the soil told what was growing in each ground plot.

"This is nice," I said. "Lots of birds and bees." I dodged a bee flying in front of my face.

"Yes, my bee boxes are at the back of the garden. They are busy little honey producers. And the birds love this place. They flock to it in the spring and stay until late fall."

I nodded, taking in all the plants. Many of them had flowers with bees working on them. I was pleasantly surprised that something about the garden made me feel peaceful. I could imagine sitting out here with a good book and losing track of time.

"Do you plant the same things every year?" I asked.

"If the plant has value to me, I continue planting it. But I'm always experimenting. There's so much to learn and do with plants," he said. "It's really quite interesting. I believe each plant was put here for a purpose and I don't believe we have discovered yet what the purpose of each is. Man is just so ignorant of these things, but I have a mission to find out as much as possible about each plant."

I nodded. It was interesting, but I thought Alec might have been more fascinated than I was and I wished he were here to talk to Barnabas.

"Before you leave today, I'll get you some cuttings of things like aloe vera and chamomile. No kitchen is complete without them. The chamomile is good for digestion, as is aloe. And of course, aloe vera is also good for burns and wound care."

I nodded again. I didn't plan on having any burns or wounds, but I didn't mention that to him. I looked over my shoulder to see if Alec was anywhere in sight. I assumed Calvin would bring him by since I had Alec's car. I pulled my phone out of my pocket to text him and ask him when he would be here.

"What are you doing?" Barnabas asked, staring at my phone.

"I'm going to text Alec and ask when he'll be here. I don't want him to keep you. I know you're busy."

"This is a no phone zone," he said, still staring at my phone.

"What?" I asked. I had never heard of a no phone zone.

He put his arms out, motioning toward the plants. "This is nature. Nature should never be interrupted with man's technology."

I stared at him. "Oh. Well, I'm not trying to interrupt nature. I just didn't want Alec to be late. It would be rude."

He sighed and shook his head. "I will have to ask you to put the phone away. If you're worried about being rude, believe me, phones are rude to the plants."

For a moment I contemplated being rude to the plants and running for the car. Then I put the phone in my pocket and prayed Alec would show up soon.

"Thank you, Allie," he said and smiled at me. "I do appreciate it."

Chapter Nineteen

AFTER TOURING THE REST of the garden and the small greenhouse, I followed Barnabas back toward the shop. When we got there, he made a detour and headed toward his house. Something told me this was a bad idea. At the back door, I stopped and looked over my shoulder, willing Alec to appear. How bad would it be if I just turned and ran to the car? That creepy sense I occasionally got about Barnabas was suddenly very strong and I wasn't sure what to make of it. He had seemed eccentric, but now it seemed like something more.

"Come along," Barnabas said, standing just inside the back door of the house. "I've prepared the most amazing roast beef with spring vegetables. All the herbs I used came from my garden. You will be simply amazed. I promise."

The scent of the cooking roast beef wafted through the open door and it did smell amazing. My stomach chose that moment to growl audibly, and I followed the scent of roast beef like a shark follows the scent of blood in the water from two miles away.

The back door opened up to the kitchen and the sight of all the copper-bottomed pans hanging over the kitchen island took my breath away. It was a cook's dream. The island and countertops were done in tiny rustic yellow tiles that matched the rest of the décor perfectly.

The house was surprisingly cute and neat. He had done everything in Tuscan yellow and olive green. Delicate leaves and flowers were painted and trailed around the windows and archway leading into the living room.

"That smells delicious," I said.

"Doesn't it? Wait until you taste it. You'll be amazed!" he said, grinning.

He led me into the living room and offered me a seat. The sofa was done in olive green crushed velvet with dark wood trim. It managed to not look overly feminine, in spite of the velvet.

"Your house is lovely," I said and sat down.

"Thank you," he said. "Let me get you some tea."

He left the room, and I used the opportunity to pull out my phone. I hoped this wasn't a no phone zone because I didn't want to be rude to the roast beef. I texted Alec as fast as I could, glancing up to see where Barnabas was.

Where are you? Kind of freaked out here. Hurry up.

I tucked my phone back into my pocket before Barnabas got back, telling myself I was overreacting. Barnabas was a perfect gentleman, and Alec would be here any minute anyway.

"Here we are," he said. "I had the water on low heat on the back stove burner. I'm so delighted you could come for lunch." He set a tray with a teapot, cream, and sugar on the walnut coffee table.

"That's lovely, thank you," I said and picked up one of the cups. I poured tea into the cup and stirred some sugar into it. I took a sip and sighed. It was the best tea I had ever tasted.

"I grew the tea in my greenhouse. It's not too difficult, as long as you keep the plants from freezing," he said with a smile.

"Really? You grow tea?" I said in surprise. I shouldn't have been surprised. The guy was really into his plants. He probably grew the walnut tree for the wood that made the coffee table.

"Yes, there's nothing like freshly dried tea leaves," he said.

I smiled and held my teacup in my hands, looking around. The house was quite warm and charming. Bookshelves lined the walls and were bursting with books. There was artwork on the walls that matched the Tuscan themed décor and lovely, bright throw rugs scattered about. I was becoming jealous. My house wasn't a dumpy shack, but it was a far cry from what Barnabas had done with his house.

"Those are my botanical books," he said, noticing my gaze. "I have books going all the way back to the 1800s."

"Wow," I said. I was losing the ability to make small talk. There was something unsettling about Barnabas and I wasn't sure exactly what. I envied his cute little house and his magnificent garden, though. I was sure it took a lot of energy to produce something this nice, and the truth was, I was a little on the lazy side. I would never have a botanical garden.

"Yes, I know it's impressive. Say, did you find out anything new about that young woman's death?" he asked.

"What?" I asked, losing my train of thought.

"You know. That young woman that died at the festival. The one the pixie-looking woman was telling everyone you had poisoned. Did you poison her?"

I stared at him. "What do you mean, did I poison her?"

He shrugged and then chuckled. "It's a joke. I'm sorry. I suppose it was in poor taste." He crossed his legs and kept his eyes on me.

"I did not poison her," I said, gripping the teacup in my hands and taking a drink of my tea.

He waved away the statement with his hand. "I know that. I was teasing."

"I don't know what happened to her," I said. "Do you?"

He smiled. "Funny you should ask."

He didn't continue.

"What does that mean?" I asked.

He shrugged. "It seems like you've been asking a lot of questions about this young woman. Why is it important to you?"

"Because people were saying I poisoned her when I didn't. That's why it interests me. Why wouldn't it interest me?" I asked. I had a prickly sensation on my scalp and I thought it was time I made my exit. But Mama and Grandmama had taught me to be polite and I couldn't bring myself to bolt for the door.

"Of course," he said. "I'm being silly, aren't I?"

I took a sip of my tea and looked at the magazines on the coffee table. I needed to figure out how to get out of here without bringing shame on my near ancestors.

"Oh, you like cars?" Barnabas didn't seem the muscle car type, but I needed to change the subject and work my way out of this place.

"No. I have no interest in them. For some reason that magazine shows up every month." He shrugged. "I thought Alec might be interested, so I set them out."

I nodded. "You're right. Alec loves cars. Kind of." He only liked the one he drove, but I needed to distract Barnabas. I felt the phone in my pocket vibrate and cursed not being able to check it. I smiled.

"So, did you find out anything about the murder?" he asked again.

"We don't know if it was a murder. Not yet," I pointed out. I drank more of my tea. I couldn't get over how fresh it tasted.

"I have a hunch," he said and grinned.

"Do you think I could get some milk for my tea?" I asked. "Cream is so heavy."

"Of course," he said. He jumped to his feet, set his cup on the coffee table, and disappeared into the kitchen.

I set my cup of tea down and pulled the phone out of my pocket. I had a text from Alec.

Be there soon.

I groaned.

"Do you have that phone out again?" Barnabas asked. He had a small silver pitcher in his hand and he set it down on the coffee table.

I stared at him. "Oh, Alec texted me. He said he'd be here in a minute." I felt sick to my stomach. Barnabas was creeping me out. Alec could think I was paranoid. I didn't care. I had to get out of here.

"Oh, good! Lunch will be ready any minute now," he said. "Please, drink your tea."

I poured milk into my tea and took a sip. "That's good," I said and smiled at him. "You know, I'm not feeling well. My stomach is a little upset. I think I might have to pass on lunch."

"No problem," he said. "I've got just the thing. You sit tight."

I sighed and took another sip of my tea. Of course he would have a remedy for an upset stomach. He was the king of herbal remedies. If I told him I was having a heart attack, he'd have a remedy for that and wouldn't dial 911. I'd be a goner. I pulled my phone out again and texted Alec.

I need you now!!!

Barnabas was back sooner than I thought he would be. I was feeling sleepy, and I shook my head to clear it.

He took one look at the phone in my hand and "tsk tsk'd".

"Do you like your tea?" he asked.

I nodded. My eyes felt heavy, and I yawned.

"Good, try this elixir. It will fix your stomach right up."

I took the tiny demitasse cup he held out and smelled it. "That smells terrible."

"But it will help you. Medicine isn't supposed to taste good."

I looked into his smiling face and took a sip. The noxious liquid curdled my stomach and I spit it back into the cup. "No," I said, shaking my head. I put the cup on the coffee table. I wasn't drinking whatever was in that cup.

Somehow Barnabas had moved to stand behind me and I suddenly felt my arms being restrained. I couldn't figure out how he had gotten behind me without my noticing him. I tried to squirm away from him, but for a skinny man, he had a vise-like grip.

"Just hold still," he said.

Chapter Twenty

MY HEAD ROLLED BACK on the sofa and I tried unsuccessfully to force my heavy eyes open. Where was I? Had I fallen asleep? I shook my head and tried to rub my eyes, but found I couldn't move my hands. My eyes popped open.

"Hey," I mumbled.

Barnabas sat on the coffee table in front of me.

"You poor, silly woman," he said. "If you had shut your mouth, you wouldn't be in this predicament."

"What are you doing?" I slurred. My head felt like it weighed a hundred pounds. Where was Alec?

"I can't let you continue your little investigation into Tessa Brady's death. Sorry." He poured something from a bottle and onto a spoon. "Now open wide."

"No!" I groaned.

He came at me with the spoon and I shook my head from side to side.

"Stop it," he said and put a hand on my head to hold it still.

I fought harder, thrashing my head back and forth. "Get away!"

"Stop that," he said and pushed down on my head. He had a vise-like grip and I screamed.

"Let me go. Alec!" I screamed. "Alec!"

"Stop it. He isn't here." Barnabas spoke as if he were trying to calm a child. "Just do as I say and it will all be over soon."

"What are you doing?" I asked. Why hadn't I followed my instincts and run for the car? Darn my Southern roots and polite upbringing. Where was Alec?

"Come on now. Cooperate," he said.

The spoon came close to my lips, and I moved my head back. I pursed my lips closed and bumped the spoon with my forehead. The liquid spilled onto Barnabas' shirt and he swore under his breath as the spoon fell from his hands and onto the floor.

My hands were tied behind me and I looked around the room for some way of escape. I had to get out of here and fast.

Barnabas reached for the spoon and picked up the bottle with his other hand. "You need to be a good girl and do as I say."

I stopped struggling and looked at him. I was regaining my senses, and I needed to hold still so I could think.

"Here we go," he said, pouring more of the liquid into the spoon. He moved the spoon toward my mouth and I kicked him in the gut as hard as I could. He made an 'oof' sound and toppled over backward off the coffee table. Barnabas's string bean frame crumpled under the force of my kick. He forgot he was dealing with an athlete.

I jumped to my feet and sprinted toward the living room door, swaying a little as I went. My hands were still tied behind me and it made running difficult. I hoped I could get to the car before Barnabas got to his feet, but I wasn't sure how I would drive with my hands behind my back. We had come in through the kitchen door and I didn't know if there was a fence separating me from Alec's car if I left through the front door.

I was still unsteady on my feet and ran into a wall. I righted myself and continued on to the front door. Barnabas was getting to his feet, and I turned around so I could turn the doorknob with my hands, then turned around again and trotted as fast as my drugged feet would carry me through the door.

I could hear Barnabas swearing behind me, but I didn't stop to look as I wobbled toward a gate. It was then I realized my purse and the car keys were in the house. "Oh, no," I cried.

"Got you," Barnabas said and grabbed me by the shoulders, pinching hard.

I screamed and turned around and kicked at his legs with everything I had.

He screamed as my foot made contact with his shin. "I'll kill you," he swore as he hopped on one foot.

"Not if I have anything to say about it," I said and pushed the gate open with my foot.

"Hold it right there," I heard a voice say. I looked up to see Alec and Cal with their guns drawn.

"Alec!" I cried and stumbled into him.

He put his gun in its holster and turned me around so he could untie me. "You're safe now," he soothed. He untied me and pulled me to him.

"Where were you?" I cried into his chest.

"I'm sorry. It's okay, Allie. Everything's okay."

I could hear Cal reading Barnabas his rights, but I didn't look up. All I wanted was to go home and forget I had ever heard of a strawberry festival.

Chapter Twenty-one

THERE WAS A KNOCK AT the door and I went to answer it. I peered through the peephole on tiptoe, first. I had had all the excitement I could handle for one day and I was being careful.

"It's me," Alec said from the other side.

I opened the door and stared at him. I had never been so happy to see someone as I had been earlier, not to mention right at that moment as well. He put his arms around me. "Don't go away again," I mumbled.

"I won't," he said and kissed the top of my head, holding me tight.

I gave the police my statement and Alec had deposited me in a motel room. It was 4:00 in the morning and I had dozed off and on, never falling into a deep sleep. I was exhausted. I had missed the remainder of the last day of the festival. I didn't care. Festivals were not for me.

"Did he kill Tessa?" I asked. I knew he had, but I wanted confirmation.

"He confessed after a few hours of applied pressure," Alec said. We sat on the sofa and I snuggled up to him.

"I'm glad you showed up when you did," I said.

"Me too. Cal and I had gone back to the station. After you texted me, the toxicology report came back. Tessa was poisoned with Belladonna. I realized there was really only one person that would have something like that around here and you were with him. I'm sorry. I feel like I almost led you to your death," he said and kissed the top of my head again.

I sighed. "It's not your fault. You didn't know. But, he knew you were arriving soon. I don't know why he tried to kill me with you on the way."

"He was going to say you were exhausted and you went to lie down in the bedroom. Then he was going to get me to drink the belladonna. The berries are sweet and I had an interest in botanicals that might help my athletic performance. He thought it would have been easy to get me to drink something with the juice of the berries mixed in," he said. "He had become paranoid that we were talking to too many people and thought we would find him out, so he decided to stop us before it was too late."

"Wow. Why did he kill Tessa?" I was trying to take this all in, but I was having a hard time wrapping my mind around it.

"She worked for him for a short while, but quit when Barnabas became obsessed with her. Tessa didn't return his affections. So, he did what any sensible mad man would do, and he killed her."

"He does seem to have an obsessive personality," I said.

He nodded. "He said both Tessa and Tracie worked for him long enough to learn the business. Then they both quit, taking his ideas with them and turning them into their own businesses."

"But Tessa was just selling strawberry jam. Tracie sold soaps like he did. It seems like Tracie took more of what she learned and turned it into a business, not so much Tessa," I pointed out.

"Barnabas sold jams at his shop. Apparently he had his own secret recipes that he claims Tessa stole after breaking his heart. She was his love obsession and she rejected him. So, he made one of those famous smoothies of his and put belladonna in it. She drank it, then indulged in one of your cupcakes, and the rest is history."

"I would think the smoothie would have made her sick pretty quickly, since it didn't take long for her to collapse. I suppose she could have bought the cupcake first, then headed to his booth. I also wonder why she would drink the smoothie. She had to know he was nuts if he was that obsessed with her."

He shrugged. "He convinced her he wasn't angry with her. Rich was questioned, and he said Barnabas tried to remain on friendly terms with the girls."

"I'm tired of murderers, Alec. I mean it. If there's ever another murder, I swear, I am running in the other direction," I said sleepily. "What did he put in my tea?"

He snickered. "An herbal concoction."

"Stop it. I'm going to eat Twinkies and junk food for the rest of my life. Eating healthy is deadly."

"You just want an excuse to eat more cake," he said.

"I sure do. Can you retire from being a PI now?"

He sighed. "I guess I could open a pet store. Or something."

"It would be safer," I said, laying my head on his shoulder. "For me. Do it for me. Puppies and kittens are safe."

He smiled. "Maybe I'll just handle missing persons cases from now on. Or lost puppies."

"Okay, but if it turns out to be dangerous, you're going to have to find something else to do."

"Deal," he said. "Sorry this strawberry festival was a bust for you. On the positive side though, Lucy texted me and said they sold all the donuts."

"At least I had one good sales day," I said. "Those donuts were great."

"Yes, they were. Hey, sit up," he said.

"Why?" I asked.

He got to his feet and helped me sit up. I looked at him and he smiled.

"I wanted this to be so much more special. I had it planned. I was going to have balloons and flowers and strawberry champagne and cake, and well, it was just going to be a lot nicer."

"What are you talking about?" I asked him.

Then he got down on one knee and looked me in the eye. "Allie, I thought I liked my dull existence before you came into the picture, but I was wrong. Life with you has been anything but dull. I like this crazy little life I've been living since you appeared. I was going to wait and ask you when we got home and I could make it romantic but, everything else has been just a little crazy with us, so why wait? Will you marry me?"

I stared at him as he pulled a jewelry box out of his pocket and opened it up. He took my hand and slipped a diamond ring on my finger.

I gasped. "Is that what I think it is?" After our Valentine's Day fiasco, I wasn't jumping to conclusions. I had made a fool of myself when I assumed he was going to ask me to marry him then. I wasn't making that mistake twice. I wanted him to say it.

He nodded. "Chocolate and vanilla diamonds on a strawberry gold band. An engagement ring, to be precise. Will you marry me?"

The ring was the most beautiful thing I had ever seen. The center chocolate diamond was square and was surrounded by vanilla diamonds. The vanilla diamonds, in turn, were flanked by smaller chocolate diamonds and the strawberry gold band was the prettiest thing I had ever seen. I squealed so loud I'm pretty sure the people in the next room heard me.

"Alec! It's beautiful! Oh, my gosh! I love it! Oh, Alec! We're getting married!"

He chuckled. "If you say yes, we are."

"Yes!" I shouted. "Yes, yes, yes, yes!"

"Do you like the ring? Because if you don't, we can take it back to the jewelry store and you can pick out another one."

"Are you kidding? This is the most perfect ring in the whole world! I mean, it's chocolate and vanilla diamonds on a strawberry gold band. How could I pick out a more perfect ring?" I asked. "Look at it!" I gazed at it, admiring how the ring looked on my finger.

"I guess that'll do then," he said with a chuckle.

I threw my arms around him and held him close. It had been an awful week, but this more than made up for it.

"I get to be Allie Blanchard," I sang. Happy tears filled my eyes. How had I managed to find someone so wonderful?

He laughed again. "Yes, you get to be Allie Blanchard."

When I finished crying, I pulled away from him and looked him in the eye. "Are you sure? Are you sure you want me? I can be a pain and I'm always getting into trouble and I want you to be sure you're making the right decision."

"Stop it," he said. "I love your craziness. We'll do so much together. We'll run marathons, we'll catch killers, oh, and we'll go to France for our honeymoon."

"Oh, no, we will not go to France for our honeymoon. No. No way," I said. "I've had all I can take of French anything for a while."

"Are you sure?" he asked with a smile.

"Stop it," I said. "We will go somewhere, just not there. And no more marathons or murders. Okay?"

He nodded. "We'll work something out."

"Okay," I said and gazed into his beautiful blue eyes.

I had the man of my dreams and I couldn't think of anything that would make me happier.

The End

Sneak Peek

Plum Dead
A Freshly Baked Cozy Mystery, book 7
Chapter One

"I can hardly believe it," Lucy said. She was looking up at the brilliant blue sky, her floppy straw hat tipped back on her head. Her short blond hair poked out beneath the hat.

"Can hardly believe what?" I asked as I grabbed the beach umbrella from the backseat. It had a telescoping pole and was a perfect fit for my car. I slammed the back door and turned to her.

"The sky is such a beautiful blue," she said, looking at me and nodding. "This is the perfect day to go to the beach. You had a great idea."

"I told you the rain wouldn't last forever," I said and popped my trunk open. Lucy Gray was my best friend. We had been talking about a beach trip for days, and now that the weather had cleared, we were finally getting the chance to go.

"Oh Allie," she said, coming to stand beside me and peering into the trunk. "It looks like you packed everything but the kitchen sink."

I chuckled and picked up a beach tote and handed it to her. "I may have. I brought a sweet beach romance novel, a scrumptious lunch for both of us, and lots of sunscreen, so there's no need to hurry home today."

"You brought lunch?" she asked, reaching into the trunk to pick up another tote.

"Sure did. I made us roast beef sandwiches, potato salad, fruit salad, and apple pie for dessert. How does that sound?"

She grinned. "That sounds wonderful," she said. "You really know how to make a girl happy."

I picked up the small ice chest and slammed the trunk lid. We headed for the sand as a seagull called and swooped down near my head. "Wow," I said. "It must have heard me say roast beef sandwich."

"No, it's the apple pie they heard," she said and chuckled.

We made our way across the beach, our feet sinking into the warm sand. "I love summer. It never lasts long enough for me."

She nodded. "Not around here, it doesn't. The snow will be back before we know it."

In Sandy Harbor, Maine, we had more than our fair share of snow for a large part of the year. And while I loved the snow, as beautiful as it was, there's nothing like a Maine summer. The blue skies and the warm sun were absolutely perfect. It got hot during the summers, but not blazingly hot like in some parts of the country, and for that I was thankful.

We had decided to get an early start, and I was glad of it. This time of the morning, the beach was beautiful, pristine, and not overly crowded. We would probably stay long enough to eat lunch and then leave when the beach got crowded.

I was a runner, but the sand was giving my legs a workout. Running in the sand used to be a part of my routine, but I hadn't done it in some time. I needed to get back to it. "Where do you want to sit?"

Lucy put one hand to her forehead to shield her eyes from the sun and glanced around. "What about over there," she said pointing to an area not far from where we were. There weren't any other beachgoers there, and I thought it would be perfect.

"Looks good," I said.

Within a few minutes, we made it to the spot she had picked out, and I set the cooler down and planted the umbrella in the sand to block out much of the sun.

Lucy began spreading the two towels out, and then she sat down on one of them. "I brought a cozy mystery to read. I've been intending to buy this book for weeks, but it seemed like something came up every time I tried to go to the book store, and then it was sold out. They got a copy of it in yesterday, just in time."

"I feel like I never get enough reading done," I said and sat down. I removed my beach cover-up and dug my book out of my bag.

Lucy eyed me. "A bikini?"

I glanced at her, still covered up. "Yes, a bikini. I'm not that old. Well, I guess maybe some people would think so, but thankfully, running keeps me in decent condition." I was forty-something, and my bikini days weren't quite behind me yet. My red hair had gotten longer over the spring, so I wound it up and clipped it to the top of my head so it wouldn't blow wildly in the breeze.

She chuckled and lay back on her towel. "I don't blame you. I wish I had kept up with the running when I tried it last year, but you know how I am. I can't seem to stick to anything."

I smiled and began applying sunscreen. "Once you get into the habit, it's not so bad. It's getting into the habit that's the hard part."

"So what's Alec doing today?" she asked.

"I think he has a job with the police department. Something about a break-in down at the grocery store."

My fiancé, Alec Blanchard, had been a detective with the local police department, but at the beginning of the year, he had retired and become a private investigator. I preferred his role as a private investigator. The police chief always looked at me askance when I showed up to help Alec out on his cases. Not that I had any business doing that, of course, and I knew it, but I couldn't help myself. I was always finding myself getting involved in things that didn't concern me, much to Alec's consternation.

"There was a break-in at the grocery store? I hope they didn't get much."

I shook my head and put my sunglasses back on. "I don't think so. The alarms sounded and scared the burglars off, but they did some damage to one of the back doors."

"Is he getting much work with the police department these days?"

"It comes and goes," I said. "Sometimes they give him quite a bit, and then sometimes he doesn't hear from them for weeks." Alec would have preferred to get cases on his own, but the police work paid well, so he didn't complain.

"I guess in a way that's good, that means Sandy Harbor is safe from crime."

I chuckled. "That or people are just getting sneakier and getting away with it." My bet was on the latter.

"I guess that's a possibility," she agreed. She reached for the sunscreen and began applying it to her face and neck.

Lucy and I had been friends since I had moved to Maine from Alabama. I'd married Thaddeus McSwain fresh out of college, and we moved here to his hometown. But Thaddeus had been killed by a drunk driver eight years ago. I had written a blog on grief for years after his passing, but last year it struck me that it seemed almost as if constantly writing about grief kept me stuck there somehow. Meeting and falling in love with Alec had given me the courage to finally end the blog. I still checked on it from time to time, and there was still some traffic going to it, but it had been months since I had published anything new and the visitors were dwindling. It made me sad, but at the same time, it felt like that was the way it was supposed to be. I had grieved, probably longer than was necessary, and it was time to move on. I hoped the people I had helped were also moving on. And the new people that needed help with grieving? I hoped they would find someone to help them through it.

I lay back on the towel and opened my book. Two children laughed and screamed as they chased one another in the surf down the beach a ways, and I glanced over at them. My own children, Jennifer and Thad, had loved the beach. For a moment I felt a twinge of something bittersweet as I watched the girl and boy play. Thaddeus had loved the beach as well, and we spent nearly every weekend during the summers here when the kids were little. But Thad had grown up and was in college in Wisconsin, and Jennifer was at a college an hour away from here. Being a homebody, she made frequent trips home. But because Thad was so far away, I didn't get to see him nearly as much.

Lucy yawned. "Excuse me," she said with a chuckle. "The sun feels so good I could just about take a nap."

"It's wonderful," I said and glanced again at the two children playing. Alec didn't have any children, and he seemed content in that. He'd had a failed marriage years ago and said he had never met anyone that he wanted to be with until he met me. It was sweet, but I wondered if deep down he missed not having a family.

Lucy scooted around on her towel.

"What are you doing?" I asked, looking over at her.

"I can't get comfortable," she said. "I should have smoothed out the sand before I laid the towel on top of it."

I chuckled. "Sand is sneaky that way. You better keep an eye on it or it will end up in your swimsuit."

She moved the towel over and began smoothing out the sand again and then laid the towel back down on it. "Now then, that should do it."

"You should do that for me, too," I said as I scrunched down on my towel, trying to force the sand to move beneath me.

"Before we leave I want to stop by the candy store. I want saltwater taffy."

"A trip to the beach isn't complete without a trip to the candy store," I agreed and turned the page of my book. "I wouldn't mind getting some of those big bonbons that Bing's has." I had a candy addiction, and for the most part I kept it out of the house, but a trip to the beach meant a trip to the candy store.

"Do you know what you should do? You should make candy," she said, looking over at me. "Think about it. It would give your business a whole new avenue for sales."

I chuckled. "That's a no on that one. I've made candy from time to time, and it's a lot of work. Very exacting work." When I'd closed down the blog, I'd begun baking desserts for a local restaurant, Henry's Home Cooking Restaurant. I enjoyed doing it, but as soon as I got started, a fancy French restaurant opened up in town, selling French pastries. It put a dent in my sales. But I started a baking blog to add to my income, and I had the insurance money from when Thaddeus had died, so I was okay financially. I did a lot of baking every day for the restaurant, and things were finally beginning to pick up again. I hoped it continued.

Lucy got up again and tried smoothing out the sand.

"What are you doing?" I asked, eyeing her.

She shook her head and looked at me, exasperated. "I don't know why I'm having trouble with the sand today. It's so uncomfortable. I must be getting old."

I chuckled. "You're not getting old. You're a spring chicken."

She laughed and shook her head. "And you're a liar."

I laughed again. Lucy was six years older than me, and that put her in her early fifties. And since I would be approaching my fifties in a few years, I knew that fifty wasn't old.

She straightened out the towel and laid it down again. Then she sat down and sighed, her eyes moving across the beach. She squinted for a minute. "Allie, what's that over there."

I put my book down and looked in the direction she was pointing. There was something large covered in seaweed on the beach. "I don't know, I didn't notice it when we first got here."

"I don't know how we missed it," she said. "Do you think it's a seal?"

"Probably so," I said, turning back to my book. Occasionally a seal that had died out at sea would wash up on the shore. I went back to reading my book, and Lucy was quiet for a minute.

"You know Allie, I don't know that's a seal out there."

I put my book down and looked in that direction again. She was right. It wasn't shaped like a seal. It didn't appear to be as big around as a seal would be and it was longer. "I don't what that is."

"Well, I can't get comfortable here. You want to go take a look?"

I glanced at her. The last thing I want to do was go take a look at something dead that had washed up on the beach, but we had all day if we wanted, so I put my book down and sat up. "All right. Let's go take a look."

We got to our feet and headed in that direction. It wasn't until we were a few feet away that I realized what it was. It was a body.

Buy Plum Dead on Amazon
https://www.amazon.com/
Plum-Dead-Freshly-Baked-Mystery-ebook/dp/B089LLKC45

If you'd like updates on the newest books I'm writing, follow me on Amazon and Facebook:

https://www.facebook.com/Kathleen-Suzette-Kate-Bell-authors-759206390932120/

https://www.amazon.com/Kathleen-Suzette/e/B07B7D2S4W

Made in the USA
Las Vegas, NV
30 March 2025